Home and Away

CARLY'S CRISIS

HOME AND AWAY

titles available in Armada

BOBBY AND FRANK

CARLY'S CRISIS

Home and Away

CARLY'S CRISIS

Trish Howarth

ARMADA

First published in Australia in 1989 by William Collins Pty Ltd
First published in the UK in Armada in 1989

Armada is an imprint of the Children's Division,
part of the Collins Publishing Group,
8 Grafton Street, London W1X 3LA

Conditions of Sale

1

'Stop the car,' cried Carly.

'What?' said Matt.

'I said, stop the car.'

Matt drew the car to the side of the road and stopped, right under the sign that read: 'You are now leaving Summer Bay'.

The sign seemed to sum up all the feelings that were churning in Carly's mind. Summer Bay had been home to her since she had been fostered out to the Fletchers, Pippa and Tom, following the death of her mother. Her father had beaten her before her mother's death, but the authorities were finally called in when Carly ended up with a fractured skull. Pippa and Tom had been more than just foster parents. They had shown her the love and understanding she had never before experienced.

Now she was leaving. Carly's mind was in turmoil. Was she really doing the right thing? Could she turn back now?

'Have you forgotten something?' asked Matt.

'No,' replied Carly stonily.

Without a word, she opened the car door and got out. Matt immediately grabbed his doorhandle and prepared to follow her.

'Stay here. I won't be a moment,' said Carly.

'What is it?' asked Matt, slightly bewildered.

'Nothing,' replied Carly, as she swung away from Matt and walked purposefully back in the direction of Summer Bay.

Matt watched her go, a look of concern on his face. Although he really cared for Carly, he had little idea of what she was going through. He understood that she must be a bit upset at leaving her foster family, but that was natural, and she'd soon get over it once she got to the city and took up the modelling job her father had promised for her. Matt settled back in the car and prepared to wait for whatever it was that Carly felt she had to do.

Carly walked along the path beside the road for a short distance, until she had rounded a curve and was no longer visible from the car. She reached into her pocket and pulled out a coin. Gazing at the coin in her palm, she remembered the night, not so long ago, when she and Philip and Bobby had sat in the Fletchers' kitchen, each in a flood of despair, each trying to decide whether to leave Summer Bay or not.

Philip had been the relieving GP for the town and was quite enjoying the break from city life. He had, however, always planned to go on and specialise, to become a surgeon. That was before he had the accident that had badly damaged his hand. He'd just received the medical report that confirmed what he'd feared all along. His hand would heal, but not enough to ever allow him to become a surgeon.

During his stay in Summer Bay, Philip had become very fond of Stacey Macklin, daughter of the owner of the Macklin Development Company. Stacey was looking forward to a rosy future, which included Philip and meant him staying on as GP in the quiet little town. Philip knew, deep down, that he had to do something more with his life. His big problem was that he didn't really know what, just that it involved more than settling down in Summer Bay.

Bobby Simpson was also in a quandary. For years Summer Bay's premier juvenile delinquent, she had quietened down considerably since she had started going out with Frank Morgan. No-one was more surprised than Bobby when, after the HSC exams were behind them, she was voted Student of the Year at Summer Bay High. All Bobby had wanted up until recently was to marry Frank and settle down to the type of life he had always wanted. A secure, predictable future with a wife and children always at home waiting for him.

The Deputy Principal, Mr Fisher, had approached Bobby, begging her to consider a university education. Fisher had always been Bobby's arch enemy, and she was more than a little puzzled by his sudden apparent change of heart. Her instinctive reaction had been to shun any mention of university. She didn't want to be a lawyer or a doctor anyway, or did she?

The three had sat at the kitchen table in a mood of despondency, each wrestling with the enormous questions confronting them — their futures. Carly wasn't at all sure that she really wanted to go to the city. Although outwardly she presented a tough facade, so much had happened in her short life, that she felt Pippa and Tom would be better off without her. She had brought so many hassles into their lives; it was time she tried to make it on her own. Or was she just making excuses? The promise of life in the city certainly had its attractions, not the least of which was Matt. Ever since he had gone to the city, Carly had missed him, looking forward to his visits to Summer Bay with childlike excitement.

There was also the lure of a modelling career. Her twin sister, Samantha, was a successful model and the cause of much of Carly's early resentment towards her father, who always seemed to consider Carly second best. Now that her father had promised her a career as a model, she saw a chance to prove to him and to herself that she was just as good as Samantha.

'There's only one way to settle this,' Philip had announced, drawing a coin from his pocket.

Bobby had protested — you couldn't decide your future on the mere toss of a coin!

'We've been sitting here for ages, trying to decide,' said Philip. 'It's got us absolutely nowhere. We could still be here in six weeks' time. As far as I'm concerned, I'll leave it to the fickle finger of fate.'

'Me too,' Carly had cried. 'I can't stand the strain any more. Heads we go, tails we stay!'

The silver of the coin glinted in the morning sunlight as Carly gently tossed it up and down in her palm. Her foot scuffed at the path, but her mind was a long way away. Finally, her mouth set in a firm line. She flicked the coin into the air.

'Tails . . . I go,' she muttered to herself.

Her hand darted out and caught the coin, which she slapped down on the back of her other hand. She hesitated for a second or two, not quite able to lift her hand to reveal her future. With an almost imperceptible shrug, Carly looked at the coin. Tails again . . . this meant leave Summer Bay.

Carly pulled herself together with determination. She quickly stuffed the coin back in her pocket. That was that. She'd live by the coin — it was meant to be.

With a spring in her step, she returned to the car.

'Let's get going,' she said to Matt.

'Are you sure?' he asked, a touch of concern creeping into his voice.

'What's up with everyone? I can't wait to get out of here fast enough.' Carly tossed her blonde curls defiantly and fixed her eyes on the road ahead. The road to the future.

2

Life in Summer Bay returned to pretty close to normal after Carly's departure. Most of the residents carried on their lives as usual.

Pippa and Tom, however, were becoming increasingly aware of how quiet the house was now that all their foster children, except Steven and Sally, had left. True, they now had their own baby, Christopher, and he was more than a handful, but for so long they had been one big, happy family that now things seemed strangely empty.

Perhaps it was just the fact that Christmas was nearly upon them. Carly had promised that she would come home for Christmas and, of course, Bobby was still in Summer Bay, but somehow hanging the decorations didn't seem quite the same without all of them there.

'Tom...' said Pippa.

Tom was busily engaged in trying to untangle a string of lights that flatly refused to become untangled.

'Yes, love,' he replied somewhat absent-mindedly.

'The house . . . ' said Pippa.

'What about it?' said Tom in a puzzled voice.

'There's no noise,' Pippa said quietly, as if reluctant to break the silence that engulfed the room.

'You're *complaining*?' queried Tom in a playful voice. But he knew exactly what she meant. It *was* too quiet.

'I don't like it, Tom,' sighed Pippa.

'We'll get used to it,' was Tom's reply.

'It's not the same,' said Pippa.

A little later that day, the seriously diminished family was sitting around the kitchen table.

Sally was happily drawing Christmas pictures on sheets of paper and Steven was idly watching her. Sally was outwardly a bright, normal eight-year-old. Beneath the surface, however, lurked her dreadful insecurity and a constant fear that Tom and Pippa might disappear from her life.

At sixteen, Steven was quiet and studious, with an inventive mind. The tragedy that had killed his parents had dealt him a cruel blow. Despite the security of the Fletchers's home, he still had dreadful nightmares about the fire that had claimed his parents' lives as he watched helplessly from across the road while his home burned.

Tom drew his chair up to the table and addressed the group.

'Pippa and I want to put something to the vote,' he said.

'Is this a family meeting?' Sally asked eagerly. Family meetings were always very important events.

'Certainly is,' replied Pippa.

'But hardly any of the family's here,' protested Steven.

'That's why we're having the meeting,' said Tom. 'Before we start, Pippa and I both want you, Steven, and you, Sally, to know we love you and we are very happy for our family to be just as it is now.'

'The thing is, how Tom and I feel isn't the only issue,' Pippa took over. It was obvious that Tom and Pippa had discussed the matter and were in total agreement.

'How you feel counts, too. You're used to being in a big family. Do you prefer it that way?'

'What we are saying is . . .' continued Tom. 'Would you like us to apply to foster some more kids?'

'Yes,' cried Sally immediately.

'I'm not sure.' Steven was more hesitant.

'Well, we can't exactly give Christopher a deciding vote,' said Tom. 'So let's look at the pros and cons.'

'I wouldn't mind another guy to talk to,' said Steven thoughtfully.

'Thanks,' smiled Tom.

'You know what I mean.'

''Course we do,' said Pippa.

'It would mean give and take. No more single rooms. And these kids would bring a whole new set of problems with them. We'd have to go through all that again,' pointed out Tom.

'The pros as well as the cons, Tom,' Pippa cried.

9

'Just making sure everybody knows what they're getting into, that's all,' explained Tom reasonably.

'Anyone think they need time to think?' asked Pippa, as she let her glance slide from one to the other.

Sally and Steven looked at each other quickly. They turned to face Pippa, both shaking their heads.

'Then we'll put it to the vote,' said Tom.

There was no need for a secret ballot. The vote was unanimous. Somehow the Fletcher home would again stretch to accommodate kids whose main needs in life were care and love.

A few days later, Celia was serving customers in her general store. Celia Stewart had a well-earned reputation as the town's busybody spinster. A bastion of the local Presbyterian church, she hadn't a malicious bone in her body, and often had no idea of the harm she could do with her idle gossip. Love had passed Celia by, and she just couldn't help her overriding interest in everyone else's business.

She didn't think it odd, however, when Matt strolled into the store and ordered a milkshake. Matt was a keen surfer and often came to the bay to catch the waves.

'There you go, Matthew. That's ... two ... three ... five dollars.'

'Thanks, Miss Stewart,' replied Matt.

'So, does this visit mean we can expect to see a bit more of you in the future?' enquired Celia.

'Dunno. Like I said ... I just came down to catch a few waves,' replied Matt.

'Oh, but you'll be back,' Celia responded confidently. 'Once a Summer Bayite, always a Summer Bayite. It's true you know. Our young people may go away, but they always come back in the end ... '

Matt nodded politely as he pocketed his change and turned to leave the store. Celia, however, sensed that there was more to this visit than she had at first thought. Her thirst for gossip wasn't going to be quenched as easily as that.

'Carly went straight over to the Fletchers, I expect?' Celia asked nonchalantly.

Matt appeared uncomfortable at the line the questioning was taking.

'Um ... no. Carly didn't come down,' he mumbled. He was desperate to be away from this intense probing. The last thing he wanted to do was discuss this with Celia.

'Oh?' pressed Celia.

Matt could see that there was no escape without giving Celia at least some more information.

'Um ... I don't see that much of her nowadays actually. She isn't living with us any more. She got a job as a secretary with an advertising agency and moved into a flat.'

Celia was clearly taken aback by this. 'Oh ... ' was all she could manage. As the next question formed itself in her mind, the door to the shop banged open and Steven entered.

11

Matt took advantage of the opportunity to quickly leave the counter, and Celia, and made his way to a table.

Steven's face lit up as he spotted Matt.

'Hey, Matt,' he cried, pulling out a chair and joining him at the table. 'What are you doing here? Why didn't you come up and see us?'

Matt glanced around the shop. Celia, who had obviously been listening with great interest, immediately reacted with embarrassment. She lowered her head and pretended to be absorbed in some work at the counter. Matt turned back to face Steven and spoke very softly.

'I didn't come up to the house because I didn't want to run into Tom or Pippa.'

'Why?' Steven asked.

'I'm a lousy liar, mate. They're bound to ask me about Carly, and I wouldn't know what to tell them,' replied Matt.

Steven's face assumed a 'here we go again' look. 'What's she done now?' he asked in a weary voice.

'Well, you know she's moved out of our place? The wonderful modelling job never came off either — her dad let her down again,' said Matt.

'Yes,' replied Steven, 'she rang Tom and Pippa.'

'Well, she's got in with this really wild group — I mean they're *bad news*.' Matt was obviously not enjoying this, but he pressed on. 'They've got her running around pretending to be her sister.'

'Oh, what?' exclaimed Steven.

'They get into all the top nightclubs 'cos everybody thinks she's Samantha,' Matt went on.

Steven sighed and shook his head sadly. Carly never changed.

'I went a couple of times — you know, to keep an eye on her,' said Matt. 'Too wild for me, mate...'

Steven didn't reply, and Matt shifted uncomfortably, unsure what he should do next.

'So, should I tell Tom and Pippa or what?' he queried.

Steven thought about this for a moment. 'No, not just yet, okay? She's coming down at Christmas. I'll talk to Bobby and Frank, and we'll have a go at her then.'

A look of doubt crossed Matt's face at this.

'Fair enough, but umm... are you really sure she's going to be here for Christmas?'

The question threw Steven completely. It had never occurred to him that Carly wouldn't come home for Christmas.

3

Steven couldn't get rid of a nagging worry about Carly following his conversation with Matt. He knew what an absolute twit she could be and was genuinely concerned that she had got herself into real trouble. When Bobby and Frank announced their intention of going to the city, Steven saw an opportunity and asked if they'd mind giving him a lift to Carly's.

'Keep your eyes on the road, will you,' Steven teased Bobby as she drove them slowly down a dingy backstreet, searching for the number of Carly's block of flats.

'Forty-nine,' announced Bobby with satisfaction. 'That's it.'

Silence fell over the group in the car as they surveyed the almost derelict building. It was obviously a block of flats, but the area had long since ceased to be even lower class. It was definitely bordering on slum.

'Bit of a dump,' remarked Bobby.

'Maybe she can't afford anything better,' said Steven defensively.

Frank agreed. 'It's her first job. She's not gonna be in the penthouse bracket yet.'

'Why settle for this though?' said Steven. 'What's she trying to prove?'

'That she can make it on her own,' said Bobby firmly.

'She should've waited. This is a lousy way to start off.' Steven did not appear overly confident as he got out of the car. 'Well, here goes.'

'See ya back here,' called Bobby as she let out the clutch and pulled away from the kerb at a speed never envisaged when that narrow street had been constructed.

As he approached the front door of the flat, Steven hesitated. It was slightly ajar.

'Hello,' he called tentatively. 'Anyone home?'

As there was no answer, he pushed the door open and entered, calling, 'Carly.'

A disembodied voice from what was presumably a bedroom called out, 'Haven't you gone yet?'

Steven was more than a little startled as he turned and was confronted by the owner of the voice, Carly's flatmate, Annabel, who appeared, adjusting a carelessly thrown on robe.

'Didn't you hear?' she said, not even bothering to glance up and see who she was talking to. 'I said I'd call you tomorrow . . .'

At last she looked up and stopped suddenly as she regarded Steven with suspicion.

16

'Who the hell are you? How'd you get in?'

'The door was open. I'm Steven Matheson.'

'Am I supposed to know you?' queried Annabel. She was barely awake and seemed almost totally disoriented.

'No, no,' replied Steven awkwardly. 'I'm from Summer Bay. I'm a friend of Carly's.'

Annabel nodded, unimpressed. 'Shut the door, will you?' she called, as she headed for the kitchen. 'She's not up yet.'

'Do you mind if I wait?'

'Please yourself,' came the offhand answer.

Steven stood uncomfortably in the middle of the room and quietly surveyed the flat. There were a couple of slices of left-over pizza still lying on the remains of a greasy carton and empty wine and beer bottles littered the floor. Ashtrays had long since reached capacity and were spewing their contents over drink-stained coffee tables and the threadbare carpet.

'Would you like a drink?' enquired Annabel, appearing from the kitchen, pouring herself a slug of cheap white wine from the dregs of a bottle.

'Think there's some coffee, if you want,' she continued, as Steven hastily declined the drink.

She lit up a cigarette and made a half-hearted attempt to clean up. 'Sit down,' she threw over her shoulder to Steven.

'We had a bit of a wild night,' she went on, indicating the state of the flat. 'Few friends round after Dino's finished.'

'Dino's?' queried Steven.

'It's a club,' Annabel answered sarcastically. 'You know, music, flashing lights!'

'Right.' Steven didn't know how to answer this.

'So — what're you doing in town?'

'Just came to see Carly. See how she's doing.'

Annabel snorted. 'You don't need to worry about Carls. She's having a ball. She couldn't have moved up at a better time... with all the Christmas parties and everything. She's made heaps of friends.'

'Thought she might be lonely,' muttered Steven.

'Lonely! She hasn't got time to be lonely. There's always somebody around... always somewhere to go... there's a bit more action here than... what's it called, Summer Bay?'

She spun round and headed for the bedroom. 'Make yourself at home,' she called. 'Carls'll surface. Don't know in what condition, but she'll surface, eventually.'

Steven was glad when Annabel left. He was feeling rather stupid sitting in the grotty flat, talking to her. He got up and made his way to the kitchen. Eventually he discovered a solitary tea-bag and a kettle and soon had the makings of a cup of black tea.

Annabel reappeared from the bedroom, this time dressed to go out. The improvement was only slight as far as Steven was concerned. She was tidier, but still tarty.

'You still here?' she flung at him.

Steven smiled politely at the absurdity of the question.

18

'Might like to do the dishes while you're waiting. Finish your tea first, though.'

'Thanks.'

At that point Carly entered the living room, looking decidedly the worse for wear. She seemed afraid to open her eyes and it was apparent that if she moved her head more than a centimetre in either direction it would be in danger of exploding.

'Annabel,' she called. 'Where are the Beroccas? I feel like someone dropped a boulder on my head.'

'We've run out,' replied Annabel from the kitchen.

Carly lowered herself gingerly into a chair as Annabel and Steven entered the room. At first she didn't notice Steven.

'Oh, what a night. Did I enjoy it?'

'If you can't remember, you must've,' Annabel said brightly.

'Ring the office and tell them I'm sick, will you?' groaned Carly, still unable to open her eyes and unwilling to focus her attention on anything other than her splitting head.

'Do your own dirty work,' replied Annabel. 'I'm going out. Catch you later,' she called as she grabbed her bag and headed for the door. 'See ya, Steve. Don't forget the dishes.'

At the mention of Steven's name, Carly's eyes flew open. She was obviously embarrassed.

'What're *you* doing here?'

'I came up with Frank and Bobby. Thought I'd call in and see how you were getting on.'

'Oh?' Carly headed for the kitchen where she scrabbled around looking for the coffee. 'And what's the verdict?'

'The place is a bit grotty,' Steven replied, tentatively.

'Typical bourgeois values, Stevo,' Carly threw at him nonchalantly. 'I like it like this. I'm having a fantastic time.'

'Tom and Pippa send their love. They miss you. We all do.'

'I haven't had much time to miss anybody,' Carly rushed on, terrified that Steven might realise how much his visit had affected her. 'I work all day and I play all night. Never thought I'd thank my sister for anything. She's always used me . . . but now I get to use her. I just pretend I'm Samantha, and the doors open. I'm an instant celebrity.'

'And your friends cash in on it,' commented Steven.

'Why not? You have to take what you can get, Steve. There are no handouts in this life.'

'Matt's worried about you,' Steven began. 'Why did you leave his place?'

'Because that isn't my scene any more,' replied Carly. 'I've outgrown Matt. And his parents tried to play the heavy. I couldn't hack it.'

'Do you really like all this?'

Carly lost her cool. 'Yes,' she snapped. 'I really like all this! Why is that so hard to believe?'

'How can you live here? It's a dump.'

'You have to start somewhere, and I'm doing very nicely thank you. I have a job and stacks of friends. I'm

20

hardly ever home anyway, so who cares? I'm not missing out. I can buy what I want, go where I want. I have real independence for the first time in my life.'

'Are you coming home for Christmas?' Steven asked quietly.

'Don't know. I don't think so. There's so much going on here.'

'Tom and Pippa'll be disappointed.'

'They'll have a full house as usual,' Carly spoke quickly, trying to convince herself as well as Steven. 'I'd get lost in the crowd.'

Steven realised that the conversation was going nowhere. He could not reach Carly, or she didn't want to be reached. Was she really having such a good time?

A car horn sounded from the street below, and Carly crossed to the window quickly. She seemed anxious to be rid of Steven.

'There's Frank and Bobby now,' she said.

Steven turned and prepared to leave, but before he reached the door it opened and Annabel entered with another girl in tow. They were both giggling and acting most strangely. Annabel sniffed occasionally and her nose seemed to be itching.

The girls totally disregarded Steven and staggered, giggling, into the room. It was clear to Steven that they were high on something.

'How come Annabel's got the sniffles in the middle of summer?' he asked Carly as they stepped onto the landing outside the flat. 'She's on something, isn't she?'

Carly chose not to reply to this. Steven went on, 'Don't let her talk you into anything.'

'I have a mind of my own, okay?' snapped Carly. 'I don't use drugs. Now, get going, will you. You don't understand this scene.'

Steven turned to go as the car horn sounded again, impatient this time. 'No, I guess I don't,' he replied.

That evening, after Annabel and her friend had gone out, Carly was alone in the flat. She idly picked up the framed photo of the Fletchers that she hadn't looked at since she moved in. A shadow of disillusionment crossed her face.

4

Christmas morning dawned bright and clear. There was an air of excitement and Christmas joy as the family gathered in the living room, with Sally dancing around begging to be allowed to open her presents.

There were smiles and hugs all round as the gifts were distributed. Sally paused under the tree where two lonely parcels remained, unopened.

'Can I open these?' she asked.

'No, sweetheart, they're for Carly.'

'She'll be here later,' said Tom cheerily.

Bobby and Steven exchanged uneasy glances. 'Bit early for Carls, Sally,' he said. 'She'll still be in the land of zeds.'

Carly was, in fact, awake. She was alone in the flat again and surveying the disarray with a little less than enthusiasm. The sound of a kettle boiling shook her out of her reverie, and she turned to pour water into a mug, already prepared with coffee.

She slopped the water and burned her finger. Sucking her finger to ease the pain, she got the milk out of the fridge. As she was about to pour it into the coffee, she smelt it and realised that it was sour. Great, even the milk had gone sour on her. A born loser!

She curled up in one of the living room chairs and sipped her black coffee thoughtfully. Here it was Christmas and what was she doing? All alone with not even any fresh milk.

Her self-pity was interrupted by a knock at the door. Carly tried to cover her surprise at the sight of Matt.

'You just caught me,' she blustered. 'I was about to get ready to go out.'

'Oh,' Matt said. 'Merry Christmas. Here I brought you something.'

Carly treated Matt and the present with the same disdain, throwing the gift onto the table and making no attempt to open it.

'Actually,' Matt went on, 'I came to invite you round for dinner.'

'Well, thanks,' replied Carly. 'I've got hundreds of invitations. I just don't know which one I'll accept yet, that's all.'

Matt saw through this facade and said quietly, 'Nowhere to go, huh?'

'What's it to you?' snapped Carly. 'Who needs Christmas anyway? I'm still getting over Christmas Eve — now that was a rave!'

'Steven told me you were enjoying the good life, and it looks like it.'

'Rack off, Matt...no lectures. I bet you've been talking to Steven, the little sneak. You always were as boring as him.'

Matt was hurt, but he still felt sorry for Carly. 'Don't spend the day here,' he said.

'Why not? I like it here. It's nice and quiet when I'm not being hassled.'

Something inside Matt snapped. If that was how she wanted it, that was how it would be!

'Okay. I'm going, but my parents would be happy to see you, and you know it. You're just not big enough to admit it. Better look out, Carly, or you'll trip over your pride.'

Carly slammed the door after him and leaned against it for a moment. With a sigh, she headed for the sideboard and poured herself a generous drink, which she gulped down.

She spent a miserable day debating with herself whether she should go down to Summer Bay or not. Deep down she really longed to be part of the happy family atmosphere, but her pride would not allow her to admit that she missed them all.

Finally, she reached a decision. Dressed and looking tidier, she called a cab and sat back as the car hurtled along the road to Summer Bay.

Just before they reached the Fletcher house, Carly asked the driver to stop. She stepped out into the still quiet night. Asking the driver to wait, she walked slowly towards the house.

As she approached, the sound of mixed voices

reached her. They were singing happily but tunelessly, and she soon recognised the strains of 'We wish you a merry Christmas'.

Tears filled Carly's eyes as she hesitated. Slowly, she turned and headed back towards the waiting cab. She just didn't have the courage to go in. All that warmth and laughter would have been too much for her.

5

When the HSC examination results were finally out, Bobby couldn't believe her eyes. She had secretly hoped to do well, but was typically prepared for the worst and expecting life to deal her yet one more blow.

Her eyes sparkled when she read the formal document. She had passed — but more than that, Fisher's faith in her had proved well founded. She had more than enough marks to get to university. Old Flathead Fisher's hounding and nagging had done some good after all.

Carly's results arrived at the same time and Bobby put them to one side, quite sure that Carly would be in touch very soon, to find out how she had done. How could anyone not care about something as important as that? Although she would hate people to know, she had been waiting anxiously for the post since breakfast on the day the results were due.

Steven was still worried about Carly. Ever since his conversation with Matt, he had been unable to rid himself of the feeling that he should do something.

When the exam results arrived, Steven saw a great opportunity to check on Carly. He and Bobby agreed that they would visit her in the city and take her results to her.

When they arrived at Carly's, there was no answer to their knock. They waited at the door, unsure of whether to wait or go away. After a few minutes, Carly, very much the worse for a few drinks, staggered up the stairs.

'You must have been out there for ages,' she slurred. When Stephen handed her the envelope containing her HSC results, Carly looked at it vacantly for a few moments then giggled. 'Why didn't you just stick the stupid thing in the letterbox?'

Bobby was already becoming irritated by Carly's attitude.

'We didn't mind waiting,' said Steven. 'Thought it might be a good chance to catch up and have a rave.'

Carly regarded him scornfully. 'Really? About what?'

'Come on, Steve,' said Bobby angrily. 'We did what we came for.'

She did, however, follow a slightly staggering Carly into the flat. Carly immediately headed towards the drink cupboard and offered them each a drink.

'Aren't you going to open your results?' asked Steven as they both declined the offer of a drink.

'They're totally irrelevant, if you ask me,' replied Carly, tossing the envelope onto the table. 'I'm living the sort of life I want to live. I don't see what difference a little bit of paper's going to make.'

28

'I'll open them.' Steven reached for the envelope.

Carly snatched it back and ripped the envelope into small pieces, before throwing it offhandedly into the bin.

'We brought this too,' said Bobby coldly, handing her a parcel Tom had asked them to deliver. 'It's your Christmas present.'

Carly threw the present onto the table with the same disregard she had shown her results. She continued to mix and swallow heavy-handed drinks.

As they watched the performance, Bobby and Steven had very different reactions. Bobby was totally disgusted and impatient to be away. Steven was still concerned, feeling that there was something wrong, but not being able to do anything about it.

Bobby jangled the car keys pointedly and tapped her foot in irritation. She wanted to be off, but Carly was holding forth about her wonderful life.

As she realised that her audience was less than attentive, Carly stopped.

'Oh, but I haven't even opened my present yet, and you went to so much trouble bringing it down.'

She unwrapped the present slowly, anxious that the others would not sense the jealousy she felt at the family warmth she had missed.

'I thought about coming for Christmas,' she said. 'But everything just seemed to fly.'

With that, she pulled the Christmas present from its wrapping, revealing a top which might have been quite okay in Summer Bay, but which hardly suited the new-image Carly.

She shrieked with laughter. 'Oh no,' she cried to Bobby. 'Who picked this one ... you?'

'I've got better things to do, Steve. You coming?' Bobby said angrily, as she headed for the door.

Steven followed her uncertainly.

'You might as well have this,' Bobby snarled at Carly through clenched teeth. 'It's an invite to me and Frank's wedding. Don't bother comin' if you don't feel up to it. And go easy on the turps, will you. I grew up in a house drownin' in the stuff.'

With that, Bobby stormed out, slamming the door behind Steve and leaving Carly to her new life.

6

The shrilling of the telephone interrupted Pippa's breakfast preparations.

'Hello, Pippa Fletcher ... yes ...'

Pippa listened with growing alarm as the caller explained that he was a doctor from a large city hospital, and that she had been listed by a patient as next-of-kin.

Pippa's mind raced. She said distractedly, 'Not next-of-kin. No. Foster parents ... Why, what's happened?'

Her face paled as she listened to the unknown voice on the other end of the phone.

'Oh, my God. When? Yes. Yes, of course. Thank you.'

Pippa hung up the phone and returned automatically to the eggs she had been cooking. She cracked another egg into the pan as Tom entered.

'Hi,' he greeted her. 'Breakfast be much longer? I'm running late.'

'I just got a phone call,' said Pippa. 'From the city. Carly's in hospital. Some friends brought her in. She's taken an overdose.'

It didn't take long for Pippa to gather herself together and prepare to go to the city. It took rather more, however, to persuade Tom that she didn't need him to go with her.

'It's not as if she's on the critical list,' said Pippa.

'I know that ... but I should be there,' protested Tom.

Pippa's reply was close to exasperation. 'Tom...' she tried once more. 'If you're needed, I'll call, okay? What's the point in both of us racing to the city like maniacs?'

'I can't help thinking it's partly our fault, Pip,' said Tom. 'You know, our "let them make their own mistakes" approach. Maybe the poor kid thinks we don't really care.'

'We don't want to make a big drama out of this. Anyway, you can't just take a day off work,' replied Pippa.

'You'll need some moral support,' said Tom.

'I'll be fine. Steven's coming,' said Pippa.

This exchange had taken place outside the house as Pippa headed towards the car. Just as she spoke, Steven appeared from the house, dressed and ready to go.

'Stevo. I think you're a bit out of your depth here, mate.' Tom was torn between the logic of Pippa's comment about his having to go to work, and a feeling of guilt at letting her and Steven face whatever was in store for them alone.

'Why?' asked Steven. 'I know the sort of stuff Carly's been going through. I can talk some sense into her.'

32

She doesn't need pep talks,' replied Tom. 'She needs sympathy . . . and lots of it.'

'I *am* sympathetic,' Steven insisted. 'It was me and Bobby who took her the HSC results, remember? And tried to get her to come back.'

This was an argument that Tom could not refute. He shrugged in mute acceptance.

'We'll manage, Tom,' said Pippa reassuringly. 'What's the point of earning black marks with your boss? If we need you, we'll let you know. I promise.'

She patted Tom's arm and made yet another move to get in the car, impatient to be off.

Tom, however, was still full of self-reproach. 'I just can't understand it. What made her resort to drugs?'

'Who knows?' said Pippa.

'The way she was going, it was probably just an experiment that went wrong,' commented Steven.

'Well, whatever it was, us standing around and torturing ourselves isn't going to help,' Pippa said resolutely.

Tom shrugged. He knew that Pippa was right. He bent forward to kiss her on the cheek. He slapped Steven on the back and stood back to allow them to at last climb into the car.

'Call me with the news, all right?' he called.

With a sigh of relief, Pippa and Steven fastened their seatbelts, anxious to be away. Pippa released the clutch a little more quickly than she might normally and the car leapt forward.

■

The trip to the city was spent in strained silence. Neither really wanted to talk about what they might find or about why Carly had ended up in hospital. Each wrestled with their own thoughts. Pippa was careful to remain within the speed limit — the last thing they needed right now was to be booked for speeding.

As soon as they entered the hospital, the smell of antiseptic assailed them. A very busy nurse in a crisp blue uniform directed them to Carly's bed.

Pippa approached the door and Steven followed her. Pippa turned just as she was about to enter and said to Steven, 'Wait here. I'll see her alone first.'

Steven was disappointed, but he soon realised that Pippa's was probably the best way. Carly might prefer to be confronted first of all by Pippa. She would need that time to face up to the fact that other people were now involved. He found a relatively comfortable chair in the waiting room and picked up a magazine.

Carly lay propped up in bed, her blonde hair straggling across the pillow. Her eyes were closed and her face was pale and drawn. Pippa was shocked at her appearance. How could such a vibrant and lively girl have come to this? She moved quietly to the bedside and gently called Carly's name.

Carly weakly opened her eyes. Her face was blank for a fraction of a second, and then recognition dawned. In one fluid movement, she sat up and threw her arms around Pippa's neck.

'Darling, how are you?' asked Pippa.

Carly sobbed, all the anguish of the last few months finally released.

'Pippa. Pippa,' she cried. 'I can't bear it. I've made such a mess of everything. I'm so unhappy.'

Pippa listened quietly as, between sobs, Carly related the whole saga of her misadventures in the city.

'It was fantastic to start with. Annabel put an ad in the paper for a flatmate, and I answered it. She was really stoked when she saw how much I looked like Samantha. She got me the job at the advertising agency and I met all her friends. They were really hip. It was great.'

Pippa's look showed that she was not so sure about this, but she was silent as Carly continued.

'We'd go out every night, and we always got into the VIP bar at clubs and discos 'cos they thought I was Samantha. It was fantastic. All these guys would try and chat me up, and buy me drinks and stuff. I had a great time.'

As she paused and sucked in a deep breath, Carly thought about what she had just said. It sounded so shallow. All that time she had been trying to convince herself that she was enjoying life, unwilling to admit that, yet again, things weren't going quite right.

Pippa broke into her reverie. 'But the novelty wore off after a while?' she prompted.

With a shuddering breath, Carly continued sadly. 'I *was* the novelty. They lost interest and dropped me. Annabel stopped asking me out, or told me to steer clear of the flat for the night, so I'd go and see a movie or something, or drop in on one of the others. But I could tell they didn't want me around any more.'

'They sound like a charming collection of people,' commented Pippa sarcastically.

'That's not the worst part,' admitted Carly. 'I knew Annabel took drugs. Most of them did it. They offered it to me heaps of times, but I didn't try it, 'cos I didn't need it like they did. I was enjoying myself anyway, in the beginning at least.'

Carly hesitated. 'But then I saw Annabel sell some stuff to a girl I'd never seen before. In the loo at this club we were at.'

Pippa tried to mask the shock she felt at these words. 'Annabel's a dealer?' she asked.

'Yes,' replied Carly. 'I asked her about it. We had a big fight. She said I was a boring kid with a country town mentality. And so I tried it. To prove I wasn't.'

'That wasn't the brightest thing in the world to do, Carly,' said Pippa. 'The doctor said you had a violent allergic reaction. You could have died.'

'I thought I *was* dying,' sobbed Carly. 'It was an awful life, Pippa. Such horrible, horrible people.'

Tears filled Pippa's eyes as she stroked Carly's hair. 'Why didn't you get in touch? We could have helped you.'

Carly didn't look up, but her head was shaking from side to side. 'You're always helping me!' she cried. 'I'm sick of screwing everything up. I couldn't stand the thought of all the "I told you so's".'

'No-one would have said "I told you so",' Pippa

replied. 'We missed you. We would have been so happy to see you.'

'It was awful when Bobby and Steve came up.' Now that she had started, Carly seemed to want to go on and on. 'I really wanted to tell them then how horrible it was. But I couldn't. So I acted like I was too cool to be bothered with them. They must think I'm such a jerk.'

Pippa gently lifted the girl's head and looked closely at her, forcing Carly to look into her eyes.

'It's up to you what they think,' she said quietly, but firmly. 'If you take a good look at yourself and admit the mistakes you've made, they'll be with you all the way, Carly. You know they will.'

Carly closed her eyes. It was great to be surrounded by love again. How nice it would be to simply rest on the shoulders of those who cared. Oh, why had she waited so long? Why hadn't she admitted that she was wrong?

When she opened her eyes, there was a new hope. She looked clearly at Pippa and smiled slightly. It wasn't going to be easy, but at last Carly felt she could come home.

She threw back the covers and slowly went about, gathering her things together. Obviously still weak, Carly dressed and gave her hair a half-hearted brush. She regarded herself in the mirror without much interest. There was a long way to go before she could be said to be herself again.

Pippa watched her move around, realising that she was still far from well. 'Okay?' she asked.

Carly gave Pippa a resigned nod. Everything had to be faced now. She couldn't hide any more.

Pippa went to the door and called to Steven. 'You can come in now, Steven.'

Steven appeared at the door, trying to look annoyed at being kept outside.

'About time,' he said. 'That corridor's really depressing.'

Carly braced herself for his appraisal. Steven's eyes swept her and took in the pale, sad face and the bedraggled clothes and hair. He tried not to let his shock show on his face, but he was afraid he was losing the battle.

'Hi,' said Carly slightly timidly.

'You look terrible,' blurted Steven.

'Thanks,' replied Carly. 'I feel terrible.'

Steven's feelings were still very confused. He loved Carly like a sister, but she had hurt him badly when he had gone to see her in the city, and he was still smarting.

'No wonder, if you're going to go sticking illegal powders up your nose . . . ' was his retort.

Pippa decided that this had gone far enough. She knew that Carly was walking a very thin line, and if Steven kept on, she might retreat and withdraw the hand she had held out for help.

'Thank you for the public health warning, Steven,' Pippa said briskly. 'But save the postmortems for another time, all right? You two go and have a coffee or something. I'm going back to the flat to get Carly's things.'

'You're coming back with us?' asked Steven, looking up eagerly at Carly. His hurt anger had evaporated. This was the old Carly, the real Carly.

'Yes,' replied Carly, watching his face carefully to gauge his reaction.

She needn't have worried. Steven's face was all smiles as he replied, 'Great.'

Carly turned to Pippa. 'I'll come with you,' she said. The last thing Carly wanted to do was return to that hateful flat and meet Annabel again. But she felt that it was too much to expect of Pippa.

'Why?' said Pippa sharply. 'I'm sure you and Annabel can spare the fond farewells.'

Carly heaved a sigh of relief. It was so good to have Pippa in control again, so easy to just do as she was told.

'See you back here then,' called Pippa as she ruffled Carly's hair fondly.

After she had left, an awkward silence descended on Carly and Steven. Eventually Carly spoke.

'You were right. You and Bobby,' she said.

'You don't have to say that,' responded Steven.

'It's true. You were right. I was wrong. Okay? I got into a bad crowd. I admit it. They were just a pack of good-timers.' An edge of defiance had crept into Carly's voice. Why couldn't he accept an apology when one was offered?

'I never said there was anything wrong with having a good time,' protested Steven. 'You're making me sound like a wowser.'

There was another awkward pause. 'I don't mean it like that,' said Carly. 'Was I really unbearable those times you came up?'

Steven shrugged. Without looking her in the eye, he mumbled, 'Yes.'

He raised his eyes to see what effect this had had on Carly.

Her eyes softened. 'Thanks for not giving up on me,' she whispered. 'You're a good friend, Stevo.'

Steven moved towards her and, with relief, Carly opened her arms and fell into his brotherly embrace.

Feeling that the emotions were running dangerously high, Steven pulled away and regained his composure.

'Come on,' he said. 'I'll buy you a coffee in the cafeteria.'

Carly smiled. Life seemed to be returning to a comfortable normality.

7

Pippa's shoulders were squared resolutely as she approached the door to Annabel's flat. She knocked briskly on the door and waited impatiently for a reply.

Annabel had been lounging on a sofa, smoking heavily and leafing distractedly through a magazine. She jumped involuntarily at the loud knocking. She stubbed out the half-smoked cigarette in the overflowing ashtray and, without making any attempt to rearrange her dishevelled clothing, made for the door.

'Yes?' asked Annabel sulkily as she surveyed Pippa.

'Annabel Hayes?' asked Pippa coldly.

'Who wants to know?' replied Annabel without much interest.

'Pippa Fletcher,' said Pippa.

'Who are you?' Annabel asked, slowly realising that this woman might mean trouble.

'I'm Carly Morris's foster mother. I want a word with you.' Pippa didn't wait for a response this time. She pushed Annabel aside and marched into the room.

Pippa could contain herself no longer. All the anxiety and concern for Carly turned to blind anger as she confronted this girl. Annabel maintained a curt and dismissive manner, but underneath, fear was starting to worm its way into her mind.

'What's this got to do with me?' she asked sulkily.

'You were the supplier,' said Pippa.

'So?' Annabel replied with a shrug of her shoulders. 'I didn't force-feed her. It was Carly's choice.'

Pippa's rage continued. It was all she could do not to shout at this insolent girl. 'She was out of her depth in the big city. And you didn't offer her any support or friendly advice. Nothing. You just plied her with drugs.'

'It's her life. She does what she likes. Why should I care?' said Annabel.

'Yes,' continued Pippa. 'Why should you care? Carly paid the rent. She was a laugh for a few weeks. A bit backward because she wouldn't try the drug scene. But never mind. You'll change her mind about that soon enough ... which you did.' Pippa paused for breath. 'And it almost killed her.'

Annabel attempted to lift her head and look defiant. 'I don't have to listen to this.'

'You *are* going to listen, whether you like it or not. I really don't care if *you* end up in some gutter somewhere because of your revolting habit. But when you start ...'

Annabel could contain herself no longer. The best form of defence was attack as far as she was concerned.

42

She put her hands on her hips and glared at Pippa.

'Have you finished?' she interrupted.

Annabel hadn't bargained on Pippa in full flight, however. There was no stopping Pippa when she felt that one of her family was threatened.

'I haven't started yet,' she was almost shouting now. 'People who use drugs should have their heads read. They're irresponsible enough. But dealers are the *scum* of the *earth*.'

Annabel found it almost impossible to withstand this onslaught. With a lot less confidence she said, 'I don't deal.'

'Really?' Pippa remarked, dripping sarcasm. 'I'm sure the police will be glad to hear that.'

'What are you talking about?' Annabel was instantly wary.

'They're on their way here.' Pippa was so angry she was barely aware of what she was saying. Sensing fear in her opponent, she said the first thing that came into her mind.

'You called them?' asked Annabel.

'Yes,' said Pippa.

Small beads of sweat had begun to form on Annabel's forehead. This self-righteous bitch had to be lying. It was all a bluff... wasn't it?

'They won't find anything,' she almost mumbled, her confidence rapidly dissolving.

'I hope not,' Pippa went on. 'For your sake. A young woman spent last night in hospital after taking drugs you gave her. The police are very interested, believe me.'

43

Annabel was visibly shaken. Her eyes darted around the room in a nervous fashion, although as far as Pippa could see there was no evidence of anything illegal lying around.

Deciding that she had made her point, Pippa briskly asked Annabel which room was Carly's. Annabel seemed incapable of speech at that moment and dumbly pointed to a door leading off from the room.

Pippa was not surprised at the state of the bedroom as she surveyed the unmade bed and piles of discarded clothing filling every available space. She knew what teenage girls were like and guessed that, without her to hound and nag, Carly had reverted to her old habits.

On top of the one wardrobe, Pippa located two large suitcases and briskly proceeded to pack up Carly's belongings. Time enough to sort it all out when we get home, she thought to herself.

As she collected the assorted make-up and various earrings from the dressing table, Pippa realised that she had heard the toilet flushing. In fact, the toilet had flushed several times, barely allowing the cistern to refill each time. Pippa paused in her packing, and a slow, satisfied smile spread across her face.

As Pippa emerged, struggling with the two heavy suitcases, Annabel appeared from the bathroom, her face a mask of fury.

'Destroying the evidence?' asked Pippa casually.

'You were bluffing,' replied Annabel. 'The cops would've been here by now.'

'They'll be here. Sooner or later. They'll catch up with you.'

A flush of colour infused Annabel's face as she realised that it *had* all been a bluff. Two thousand dollars' worth of cocaine had just gone down the loo because of this interfering woman.

'Do you know what you just cost me?' she raved.

'Ten years off your life?' said Pippa calmly.

'Ha, flamin' ha. You owe me about two grand.' Annabel was almost beside herself.

'I don't owe you a thing. That stuff you peddle is lethal, not to mention illegal. Now it's where it belongs. Down the toilet.' Pippa's anger had now turned to disgust. How could people do this to themselves, let alone to others?

'You'll pay me back,' Annabel threatened.

'You don't frighten me, young lady,' said Pippa as, she reached for the doorhandle. 'Your terror tactics might work with the impressionable kids you exploit, but not me. Goodbye.'

With that, she walked through the door, closing it very firmly behind her.

Annabel stared after her. She was furious at having allowed Pippa to bluff her into disposing of all that valuable cocaine.

'We'll see,' she muttered darkly.

8

Back in the hospital room, Carly had disappeared. Muttering a half-hearted excuse about having to get something, she had left Steven perched on the edge of the bed, flicking through a magazine.

He glanced up with relief as Carly came bursting back into the room.

'Where did you get to?' he asked.

'Nowhere. Just had to get something,' was the reply.

'Any sign of Pippa?' Steven enquired.

Carly nodded. 'She's coming now.'

As if on cue, Pippa came hurriedly into the room.

'Come on, you two. Quick. I'm double-parked,' she panted.

'You took your time,' said Steven, as they moved to collect the last of Carly's belongings from the room.

Pippa turned to face Carly. 'I called your loveable flatmate's bluff,' she said.

'What?' said Carly.

'I told her the police were on the way. She flushed the rest of her drugs down the loo,' explained Pippa.

'Good one, Pippa!' exclaimed Steven.

'What did she do when the police didn't turn up?' Carly asked with a note of alarm.

'She acted tough,' replied Pippa. 'Told me I'd pay. Empty words. What could she do? Come on. I'll get a ticket at this rate. I phoned Bobby. She knows we're on our way.'

Steven turned and began to follow Pippa's footsteps along the corridor, towards the exit.

'I'm nervous, Steve,' said Carly quietly.

'What about?' asked Steven.

'Going back,' replied Carly.

'You don't have to be.' Steven sounded reassuring.

'It's going to be hard facing Bobby. And what about people like that beastly Alison Patterson from school?'

Steven rested a hand on her arm. 'They'll be okay,' he promised.

'No,' said Carly. 'I've been such a jerk. And they'll never let me forget it.'

'Stop saying that,' Steven replied sharply. 'We've got to go. Pippa'll kill us.'

Carly hesitated yet again. It had been so easy a little while ago to throw herself on Pippa and pretend that life would be normal again. Her confidence had all but evaporated now as she realised that not everyone would be as sympathetic and understanding as Pippa.

As she cast her mind nervously back to Summer Bay and its many residents, she had a sudden urge to turn and run from the hospital, back to her life in the city. At least no-one really knew who she was there, or cared.

48

As Steven headed purposefully towards the exit, he heard Carly's voice from a short distance behind him.

'I forgot something. You go on, I won't be a minute.'

Steven glanced back. He knew that by now Pippa would be sitting in the car, and he could imagine her anxiety as she scanned the street for marauding parking cops. He decided he'd better join her and hoped that Carly wouldn't be long.

Carly darted back into the hospital room. Biting her bottom lip and obviously in a distressed state, she reached into her pocket. Her hand shook slightly as she brought out a small bottle. With a furtive air, she quickly took the lid off and took a large swig of brandy.

She closed her eyes and felt the burning sensation of the liquor as she swallowed. She sighed heavily as she replaced the bottle in her pocket and turned to follow Steven.

Clearly, her high-living life-style in the city had left a terrible legacy.

9

Matt and Frank were alone in Ailsa's coffee shop, except for one customer, Judith. Most of the residents of Summer Bay were sure that the main reason why Ailsa had taken on Bobby as a partner in the coffee shop was to give Bobby something she could become really involved in.

Frank had succeeded in convincing Bobby that she should not go to the city, but should stay and marry him. Bobby was pleased to go along with him; she really loved Frank and couldn't imagine a life without him. Ailsa, however, had felt that it was a waste of Bobby's obvious talents. Despite the fact that Bobby had always been considered the town tearaway and many people thought she would amount to nothing, she had a very sharp brain, and Ailsa was convinced that the girl needed something more than a check-out operator's position to challenge her.

'I chucked in my job at the resort yesterday,' Matt was telling Frank. 'Bobby offered me more money to work here, so I thought, "Why not?".'

Frank's mind was not entirely on what Matt was saying. He was glancing around the shop, obviously looking for someone other than Judith, who was seated at a table some distance away.

'Um... where is Bobby?' he asked Matt.

'Over at the caravan park. Pippa called and said Carly was coming home, so she took a couple of hours off.'

Matt lifted the milkshake off the machine and started to carry it towards Judith.

'Oh, right,' said Frank. 'You know about Carly, then?'

'I know she's coming back, but I don't know why,' replied Matt, without a great deal of interest. 'Guess something must've gone wrong. She said she was having the time of her life last time I saw her.'

'Are you going to give her a call?' asked Frank.

'Who? Carly?'

'Yeah.'

'No way,' replied Matt as he put the milkshake down in front of Judith, who was listening to the exchange with mounting interest. When Carly had left Summer Bay, Matt had been everything to her and, as far as Judith knew, the feeling had been mutual. Something very interesting must have happened.

'Why not?' Frank was puzzled.

'Mate, with all due respect, she was so up herself in the city that I just don't want to know about her now.'

Judith smiled to herself. She couldn't wait to talk to Alison. ■

Alison Patterson, however, had other things on her mind just at that moment. The chain had come off her bike just on the outskirts of town, and she was wrestling unsuccessfully with it.

As she grappled with the chain, Pippa's car slowly rounded the bend. Pippa noticed Alison's plight and smiled.

'Do you remember the week after we first moved down here?' she asked Carly. 'Oh, no, that's right, you wouldn't. You weren't in the van.'

Carly dragged herself back from her thoughts and turned to hear what Pippa was saying.

'What?'

'When we were bringing Bobby back after she'd run off to the city,' Pippa continued. 'Do you remember that? Well, Tom saw Mr Fisher by the side of the road ... so he swerved into a puddle ... '

As she spoke, Pippa swung the wheel violently.

'Watch it!' called Steven, as the front wheel of the car hit a large puddle. Muddy water sprayed in all directions, completely drenching the hapless Alison.

' ... and splashed him,' Pippa went on casually. 'Quite accidentally of course.'

For the first time in a long while, Carly laughed. The sight of Alison, the town bitch, dripping mud and hurt pride, was too much. She laughed and laughed.

Alison could do nothing. She stood, furious, by the side of the road and watched the receding car. She caught a glimpse of Carly's laughing face through the rear window.

By the time she reached the coffee shop, Alison's anger had abated slightly, but she was still far from happy as she entered, trying desperately to dry her hair with a rather inadequate hanky.

Judith looked up in surprise at her friend's entrance. 'What happened to you?'

'Don't ask,' snapped Alison.

She turned to Matt, who was behind the counter viewing the scene with mild amusement.

'Chocolate milkshake,' she demanded.

'Sure,' said Matt, as Alison pulled out a chair and sat down heavily beside Judith.

'What a day!' Alison exclaimed.

'I didn't think you were going to be seen dead in here?' remarked Judith, wisely deciding that Alison was not about to explain her dishevelled appearance.

'Yeah, well I'm not dead, am I?' was Alison's reply. 'Anyway, have you tried one of those putrid milkshakes Celia Stewart's flogging at her place?'

Judith shook her head at this last question, and Alison went on to expand on the matter.

'Well, when you do, you'll know why I'm here. The old biddy's trying to compete, but I'm telling you she's right out of the race.'

Judith smiled. Now that Alison had calmed down a bit, she would be able to pass on the latest juicy information she had gathered.

'Hey, have you heard the gossip? Carly Morris is coming back.'

'I know,' remarked Alison with a wry look. 'Her

suck of a den-mother just drove into a puddle and drenched me.'

'Yeah?' said Judith, suddenly interested that Alison might know more about this than she did.

'They're asking for it, those Fletchers,' Alison was still fuming. 'I tell you, that whole stuck-up family is really asking for it.'

'Did you see Carly?' Judith wanted to know.

'Briefly,' said Alison.

'Why's she coming back, did she say?' Judith was eager for more.

'How would I know?' snapped Alison. 'I only saw her. I didn't talk to her.'

'How'd she look then?'

'How d'you think?'

'Daggy?'

'Mega-daggy.' Alison was warming to the subject. 'Actually, she looked like death warmed up. I reckon she got into some sort of trouble . . . '

'Oh, isn't that sad?' said Judith, in mock concern.

'Yeah, heartbreaking,' Alison said, as Matt put a milkshake in front of her. 'Thanks.'

As she watched Matt's retreating back, her eyes lost their anger and assumed a look of longing.

'That's something else Celia Stewart's shop doesn't have,' she remarked.

'Cute, isn't he?' said Judith.

Alison nodded and took a long sip from her milkshake. Her thoughts had already gone back to Carly.

'I wonder why Morris did have to come back?' she mused. 'It'd be great to find out, wouldn't it?'

Alison would give an arm and a leg to find out.

10

At the Fletcher house, hurried preparations had been made following Pippa's phone call. Bobby had done a half-hearted job of cleaning up the bedroom she would once again share with Carly. Sally had been dissuaded from hanging up the Christmas decorations. Bobby had explained to her that Carly wouldn't want people to make a fuss.

Once inside the house, Carly made her way to the bedroom to put her things away and settle in again. Opening the door, she saw Bobby sitting on her bed. Carly noted with amusement that the supposedly tough Bobby was flicking idly through a glossy bridal magazine. She was really taking this wedding business seriously.

Bobby glanced up as Carly entered the room. There was an awkward silence as the girls regarded each other, neither quite sure how to react.

'Hi,' said Bobby eventually.

'Hi.'

Carly pointed to the magazine in Bobby's hands and raised her eyebrows.

'Any jokes about me goin' all mushy and I'll flick your bra strap so hard it'll draw blood.' For all the toughness of this remark, Bobby had a warm smile on her face, and Carly acknowledged it gratefully.

'Any jokes about me and I'll do the same, only harder,' she responded.

Bobby nodded. That was fair enough.

'I see you cleaned the room up,' said Carly

'Yeah, but don't think I did it for you or nothin', all right?' Bobby was her usual tough self, seemingly terrified that someone might realise that under the brash exterior lived a warm and sensitive human being. 'I'm just practisin' for when I'm livin' with Frank. One of us has to learn to clean up.'

'Must be only a week or so till the big day.' Carly was thinking aloud. Overcome by her own problems, she hadn't spared a thought for Bobby.

'One week tomorrow,' agreed Bobby. 'And, hey, er... d'you wanna be me bridesmaid?' she added, slightly embarrassed and unsure of her reception.

'Me?' exclaimed Carly, completely taken by surprise.

'Yeah,' said Bobby. ''Cos like, for two people who reckon each other are total dags, we don't get on too bad really, do we?'

Carly thought about this for a few moments. This didn't sound like Bobby. Did she have an ulterior motive?

'Who are you kidding?' she asked suspiciously.

'What?' Bobby was taken aback. How could Carly be like this?

'You don't have to feel sorry for me...' Carly started to protest.

'I'm not!' Bobby stated vehemently.

'With a week to go, you suddenly want me to be bridesmaid?' Carly was still suspicious.

'I always wanted you to be me bridesmaid, you just haven't been around to hear me say it. And don't say "Well you could've called and told me", 'cos I sort of figured, well, gees, if she didn't come back for Christmas, she won't come back for a wedding, will she? But seein' as you're here, I'm tellin' ya. I'd like you to be me bridesmaid.' Bobby paused for breath and Carly hesitated.

'So... what d'you say?' pressed Bobby.

Still Carly hesitated.

'I only need a yes or a no.'

'I'd like to...' Carly was obviously wrestling with something.

'What's that, a yes?' Bobby was almost pathetically eager.

Inside, Carly was in turmoil. She had come back to Summer Bay, but had not really thought much about the future. At the moment, all she wanted to do was hide. A wedding would mean meeting people and presenting herself in public, something she was not ready to do yet.

'No,' she replied. 'I mean... well, I... I was hoping to lie low for a while... get over things...' she trailed off, expecting Bobby to shrug and say 'That's okay' or something. Bobby, however, was not about to oblige.

59

'You're not disappointed, are you?' said Carly rather more gently, as she could see Bobby was hurt.

'Yeah, I am,' said Bobby. 'I figured the one thing you had was guts. What's the point in hidin' out in here? So you don't want a huge postmortem on where you screwed up, fair enough, but if you want to stop people whisperin' behind your back, you gotta turn round and face 'em, don't you?' Bobby paused to stare hard at Carly. 'If you be me bridesmaid, it'll be partly for me, and partly for you. I'll be happy, and you can say to the whole town like, "Hey, so I screwed up. At least I'm not lettin' it get to me, guys." So what's it gonna be? Yes or no?'

Carly thought about this for a moment. She had to admit that there was a logic to what Bobby was saying. Despite their outward antagonism, the two girls were fond of each other, and Carly didn't want to hurt Bobby. She would do it for her sake.

'Okay,' she nodded.

Bobby's face broke into a delighted grin. 'Good on ya,' she said, grabbing her magazine and bouncing out of the room.

Alone, Carly wandered around the familiar room, rediscovering all the things she hadn't even really noticed before. She opened her case and started to put a few things away in a desultory manner. Her mind was racing and not at all on what she was doing. It had felt so good to collapse into Pippa's loving arms at the hospital, but she really hadn't thought about how hard it was going to be facing people. True, there were many people in

Summer Bay who would be pleased to see her back, and most of them would be sympathetic, but she wasn't sure she could face pity. Would things ever be the same again?

She glanced out of the window at the gathering dusk. Her nerves were jangling. During her stay in the city, she had got into the habit of having her first drink of the day about now, and with the multitude of emotions chasing each other through her mind at the moment, it was hard not to think about a drink.

She tried to pull herself together, telling herself that she didn't need one, but her eyes kept returning to the pillow where she had hidden the flask. Temptation mounted and tiny cracks started to open up in her determination.

She crossed to the pillow and extracted the flask from its hiding place. Automatically, she unscrewed the top and started to raise the flask to her lips.

'No,' she said to herself in a quiet but determined voice.

She put the flask down but couldn't draw her eyes away from it. She paused for a moment, seemingly calm, but inwardly seething.

Her determination faltered for a moment and she grabbed the flask. Quickly unscrewing the cap, she took one swig of the amber liquid. As soon as she swallowed the mouthful, she was overcome with self-loathing. How could she be so weak? Anyone would think she couldn't survive without a drink.

Clutching the flask in her hand she rushed out of the room. Fortunately, she made it to the kitchen without meeting anyone, and immediately began to pour the contents of the flask down the sink. Her nerves were screaming, but she had to prove to herself that if she didn't have any alcohol she wouldn't want a drink.

As the last drop trickled down the sink, the back door opened and Tom entered the room. Carly hastily pocketed the empty bottle and spun round to face Tom.

Tom moved across the room to give Carly a hug. 'Welcome home,' he said simply.

Carly did not reply immediately. She was torn between guilt about the drinking problem and genuine happiness at seeing Tom again.

'How are you?' he asked gently.

'Good,' said Carly, glad that her face was hidden in his shoulder.

'You're, er... all over it?'

Carly nodded dumbly. She couldn't trust herself to speak at that moment.

'Great,' Tom went on. 'That's great. It's good to see you again, love. And, er... and that's it, is it? You don't have to go on any... program or anything...?'

'Tom...' Carly began.

'I'm not criticising... I just want to know, that's all.'

'I did it once, and I got an allergic reaction. I'm not a junkie. I'm not even a user,' Carly explained carefully.

'Okay, okay,' said Tom, reaching over to give her another hug. 'I'm sorry... I love you, I worry about you... so I just wanted to know. That's all.'

That this statement was true was perfectly obvious to Carly. Tom really did care and wasn't attacking her, just concerned.

Carly nodded and smiled. Glancing at the clock she remarked, 'Must've been a long day at the office.'

'No,' replied Tom, as he gently guided Carly to the living room. 'I was only there till lunchtime. Spent the afternoon out at the resort site. I forgot what untamed nature's really like. You look at the TV commercials and think it's paradise, but up close there're mossies everywhere, and flies, and prickly things keep gettin' caught in your socks...'

They both seemed anxious to talk about normal, everyday things. Tom sat down heavily in his favourite armchair.

'Ah!' he exclaimed. 'That's better. Home at last.'

Carly, however, felt too agitated to sit down. As they continued with idle chatter, she paced the room, trying to appear as though she was just wandering, when in fact, it was a struggle for her to concentrate and stay relaxed.

Tom kept up his general conversation about the goings on at the new resort site. After a few minutes, he became aware that Carly's replies were more and more vague and that she didn't seem to be really interested. He sensed there was something very wrong.

'When did you get in?' he asked.

'Um... four maybe,' Carly jumped, as she realised that Tom had spoken to her and was waiting for an answer. 'Bit after. Not long ago. Bobby was here for a while, but she had to go back to the shop. Get this though, practically as soon as I arrived she asked me to be her bridesmaid. How about that, huh?'

'Terrific.' Tom was really pleased. 'Are you going to do it?'

'Yeah. Yeah I am,' Carly replied. Her response was jerky though and she gave the impression of being very much on edge. 'Should be fun,' she went on.

'Yeah,' she said with forced gaiety. 'So, er... how's Christopher?'

By this time, Tom was watching Carly closely. He knew something was not right, but he had no idea what it was.

'Oh, he's fine,' he responded, trying to sound as normal as possible. 'I think he is anyway. He was this morning.'

'You know I drove all the way back in the car and never thought to ask. Pippa was sitting right there and I didn't even...' Carly's speech was coming in staccato bursts. 'That's bad isn't it? Have to apologise about that... yeah.'

These remarks had been fired off as she continued to pace the room, her hands fluttering from one object to the next.

'Why don't you sit down?' Tom suggested gently. 'You're makin' me tired just looking at you.'

'No thanks, I'm fine. So what else is news?' Carly was desperate to try to keep the conversation flowing in a normal way. She was totally unaware of how unnatural she was appearing as she became increasingly more fidgety.

Tom pretended not to notice and shrugged his shoulders. 'Well, let's see... what have you missed out on...?' he began.

Suddenly Carly interrupted. 'Oh, no. What if... I just thought, Bobby isn't getting the dresses made, is she? There mightn't be enough time if... if I have to be measured and fitted and everything.'

'There's plenty of time,' said Tom calmly.

'There's only a couple of days.' A note of panic was creeping into Carly's voice.

'No, there's over a week... that's heaps of time.'

'Oh, yeah,' said Carly, seeming to calm down and throwing Tom a 'silly me' look. 'Forgot which day I was up to.'

'Are you sure you're over it all?' Tom tried again to get Carly to confide in him.

'What do you mean?' Carly was instantly on guard.

'You just... you still seem a bit strung out,' replied Tom.

Carly paused and considered what he had said. She realised how she had been acting and what she must have seemed like. With a conscious effort she pulled herself together.

'No, I'm fine. Honestly,' she said.

'There's nothing here, is there? I mean... you know, in the house. You didn't bring anything back...?' Tom's voice trailed off. He obviously thought Carly's discomfort was drug-related.

Carly managed a wry, patronising grin. When she spoke, it was lightheartedly, but in the tone one would use to a small child who'd just asked a very simple question.

'No, Tom. Nothing. I haven't been lying to you. The

truth is I'm not addicted to anything... except this family. All right?'

Tom smiled as Carly leaned over and put her arms around him. She gave him a peck on the forehead and he sighed. That was more like Carly.

'And if I look a bit washed out, it's only because it's been a fairly hectic sort of a day,' Carly went on. 'You look a bit washed out too if it comes to that.'

Tom smiled and patted her hand. He was happy to accept that explanation.

'Mind if I go for a walk?' said Carly casually. 'I'll be back for dinner.'

'No, no, 'course not. Go for your life.'

'See you soon,' called Carly cheerily, as she went out of the door.

As soon as the door closed, however, the sunny disposition vanished. Carly leaned against the door and closed her eyes. The strain of keeping up the act with Tom had been enormous, and beads of perspiration formed on her brow.

Her hand shook as she reached into her pocket and brought out the flask. She hastily unscrewed the cap and put the mouth of the flask to her lips, anticipating the calming effect of the liquor. Reality hit her hard as she remembered that the flask was empty. How could she have been so stupid as to pour it away?

Carly was getting desperate. Hating herself more with every moment, she cast around in her mind. What could she do? What had she become?

11

Donald Fisher was relaxing in his favourite chair. He was perfectly happy tonight as he lay back in his obviously masculine room, his coffee and a decanter of port within easy reach. Strains of Mozart drifted across the room as he sat with his eyes closed, savouring the peace.

This peace was rudely shattered, however, by an urgent banging at his front door. Fisher was puzzled. Who would be visiting him at this time? His curiosity turned to amazement as he opened the door.

A somewhat dishevelled Carly stood on his front doormat, a wild-eyed look on her face. She was trying very hard to keep control of herself, but only half succeeding.

'Please, sir,' she gasped to the startled deputy principal. 'Can I come in for a minute? I need your help.'

Fisher always prided himself that he gave his students a *real* education, and wouldn't ever consider turning away an ex-student in need of advice or help.

He nodded and led the way into the living room, then held a chair for her to be seated.

Carly was still having difficulty keeping her emotions in check, but she took a deep breath and started to speak.

'Coming home in the car this afternoon, I kept on hearing what you said to us at the beginning of last year. How important it was to apply ourselves ... to think about the future. "This isn't the year to live life for the moment," you said. Or something like that.'

Fisher was still puzzled by the visit. Relations between he and the Fletchers had never been particularly good. He had victimised Bobby for years, and this had caused ill-feeling between himself and the Fletchers ever since their arrival in Summer Bay. He knew he wasn't liked in the community, but, despite his self-sufficient facade, this hurt. He felt he'd done a lot for the town and received very little in return. He saw himself as a decent man of strong principle. He was, however, incapable of seeing the harm his narrow-minded attitudes could do.

'That's right,' he said. 'That's exactly what I said.'

'Well,' Carly went on, 'did I ever stuff up. And now I'm just a mess. I don't know what I can do.'

Carly was close to tears as she realised that she was on the verge of pouring her heart out to Fisher, of all people. She hung her head as she pressed on with the purpose of her visit.

'I don't even know what I got in the HSC.'

'You don't?' Fisher was genuinely surprised.

'Bobby brought the letter down . . . and I didn't even bother opening it,' said Carly.

Fisher frowned disapprovingly. How could anyone not be interested in the results of twelve years of education?

Carly continued quickly, 'I know, it was stupid. I guess I was just a bit . . .' She bit her tongue. She had nearly said a bit *drunk*. ' . . . off the air,' she finished lamely. 'And I was pretty sure I hadn't done too well anyway . . . plus I didn't think I'd ever need it.'

She paused and looked ruefully at Fisher. He had a look on his face which, under other circumstances, might have been quite amusing. He really couldn't believe that anyone could have so little regard for schooling. She continued before she lost her nerve and fled the room.

'But I really have to do something. I've got to change things. I just feel . . . so screwed up at the moment. So, if there's . . . some way I can find out what I got . . .?'

Fisher regarded her critically. 'I should have the results in my study,' he said. 'I won't be a moment.'

'Thanks,' said Carly with relief. At last he was taking a positive step.

As he left the room, Carly's eyes drifted to the table where the decanter of port was standing like a beacon. Her eyes flicked to the door which had closed behind Fisher and then back to the port. She closed her eyes for a second, hating the urge that was making her want to grab a glass and down a quick drink.

As she opened her eyes, however, they went straight

back to the port. Both the decanter and the gnawing urge within her were still there. It was taking a lot of strength to say no, and her hands shook.

For what seemed like an eternity, she gazed at the port, wrestling with the desire for a drink and loathing herself for the feeling. At last she could stand it no longer. After a quick glance at the door, she reached over and grabbed the decanter.

Just at that moment a voice came from the study. 'Ah. Here we go.'

Carly instantly replaced the decanter and settled back in her chair. Something inside her was relieved that she had been foiled. What had she come to?

'Now, let me see . . .' muttered Fisher, as he returned with a small batch of papers. 'Meads, Michaels . . . ah, Morris.'

As he read the results before him, a frown crept over his face. It was obvious to Carly that the news wasn't good. He handed it to her.

'Third name down,' Fisher pointed to the line. 'An unspectacular result, I think you'd agree.'

Carly's heart sank. What had she hoped for anyway, a miracle?

'That won't get me into anything, will it?'

'It depends what you want to do,' Fisher replied. 'I thought you wanted to try modelling.'

Carly shook her head. 'That was just a dream. I couldn't be a model.'

'Well, what do you want to do?' asked Fisher.

'I want . . .' began Carly. 'I don't know. All I know is

I don't want to do what I'm doing now. I hate it. It's nothing. I've got to get out of it. I've got to start working towards something instead of just . . . floating. I want to go to college or uni and do something, you know . . .'

Fisher considered this for a moment. 'Mmm. Unfortunately, I think college and university are out of the question.'

Carly paused slightly, then blurted out, 'Unless I do the HSC again. I can go back, can't I? Please, sir? Can I repeat Year Twelve?'

While this rather unexpected exchange had been taking place, Alison was still in the coffee shop, anxiously trying to extract some more information about what she was sure would be a great scandal.

'I was just wondering what her problem was,' she probed Matt. 'I thought Carly was a real trendoid who thought the whole city experience was just so-o-o fab.'

'She was,' was all Matt would say.

'So why's she crawled back into Summer Bay?' pressed Alison.

'I don't know.' Matt refused to be drawn.

Unseen by either of them, Bobby had entered the shop by the back door, and stood quietly, interested in the scene before her.

'Couldn't you find out?' Alison almost begged.

'I don't want to find out,' said Matt flatly.

'I bet she was almost chucked in gaol or something.

Was that it?' Alison was gnawing like a dog with a bone.

Matt lost patience. 'Alison, I don't know. Why don't you ask Carly?'

A voice from the back of the room caused them both to turn suddenly.

'Or better still,' said Bobby coldly, 'why don't you just go and stick your head down a toilet and pull the chain?'

Alison gave her a sour look and returned her attention to Matt.

'Your boss is a real class act, Matt,' she said scathingly.

'Just tryin' to use language you understand,' remarked Bobby.

'Ha, ha. That's real funny.' Alison felt she was on the losing end of this encounter, and tried in vain to come up with a really good shot. 'You're just so funny, aren't you? Well you won't be laughing for long, you dwarf.'

'Yeah?'

'Yeah.'

'And what are you going to do to stop me?'

'You'll see.'

'Oh, it's a "you'll see" threat is it? God, how many times have I heard that?' Bobby was not really proud of herself for lowering herself to Alison's level, but there was something about that girl . . .

'Yeah, well you can think it's just a threat if you like,' Alison went on, 'but I know exactly what I'm going to do.'

Confident that she had at least had the last say, Alison got up and strode out of the shop.

'What a moron,' declared Bobby. 'What did she want to know about Carly?'

'Just why she came back,' replied Matt. 'I told her at the start she'd be better off talking to you, but for some reason she didn't want to.'

'Yeah, strange that, eh?' Bobby said with wry amusement.

Matt continued wiping the tables and preparing to close the shop.

'Hey ... you spoken to Carly yet?' asked Bobby.

'Nope,' was Matt's flat reply.

'I think she'd appreciate it.'

'Let's just drop it, okay?' Matt snapped.

'You're really not gonna give her a second chance?' asked Bobby.

'Second chance?' Matt swung to face Bobby angrily. 'She had her *second* chance about February last year. If we were counting chances, we'd be in triple figures by now. She can't help herself, that's her problem. She does something without thinking, then regrets it. Then does it again, and regrets it again. So I don't want to hear about how she's really sorry this time, because I've heard it all before, and it means nothing. She's never going to change.'

12

Pippa, Steven and Sally were gathered around the table with Carly in the Fletchers's kitchen, and Tom was pottering about at the sink. Carly had related, in part, her conversation with Donald Fisher and had made the announcement of her intention to return to school this year and repeat Year Twelve.

'And there weren't any problems?' asked Pippa.

'No. He just said, "Yes, that's fine",' Carly replied.

The mood was generally optimistic, although Pippa had to admit to being surprised at this change in Carly. If the trip to the city had been a disaster in most respects, perhaps it was not a total write-off if Carly had matured to this degree. Tom fetched three glasses and, feeling that a celebration was in order, retrieved a bottle of champagne from its hiding place at the back of the fridge.

'That's wonderful,' Pippa said happily.

'Yeah, good one,' agreed Steven.

Sally was totally puzzled. 'I don't get it. What do you want to go back to school for?' Why anyone would *want* to go to school was beyond her.

'Well, Sal...' Carly explained. 'It's sort of like...I really messed up last year, see, so now I have to go back and do it properly.'

'Except none of us told her to go back,' said Tom, as he surveyed the group proudly. 'Carly just took a look at where she was at, and decided to do it for herself. And that's what I'm impressed with.' He paused and looked at Carly.

'I'm sorry if I sounded like I didn't believe you before. You obviously do have your act together, and I'm very proud of you.'

'Me too,' added Pippa.

'And it deserves a toast. Champagne!' Tom started prising the cork off the bottle.

'Right on,' cried Steven.

'You're not getting any,' said Tom.

'Why not? I've had it before.'

'When?' was Tom's immediate response.

'Phil gave me some.'

'He's a doctor. So that was under medical supervision.'

'Tom!' protested Steven.

'You're fifteen, Steven.'

'So? A minor point...'

'Exactly!' chimed in Pippa.

'Come on, half a glass. What do you say? That won't hurt me.'

'No,' said Tom firmly.

This cheerful bickering went on for several minutes. Carly didn't hear any of it. Her eyes were fixed on the champagne bottle, and the battle within her had started all over again. She knew that if she had a glass, she would want a hundred. But she did so badly want a glass. Part of her mind told her to have a glass or two, she could always stop, but the logical part of her brain knew it would be disaster.

'None for me thanks,' she said, as Tom passed around the glasses, to everyone except Steven and Sally.

'You're all right, you're eighteen,' said Tom.

'And you deserve it,' Pippa added.

Steven was still protesting. 'I'll wash the car and clean the caravans.'

'Forget it. See me in three years,' said Tom, as he passed a glass to Carly.

It took the last of her reserves of willpower to say, 'No. Thanks, really.'

'I'll wash the car, clean the caravans and mow the lawns.'

Tom looked at Carly over Steven's head. 'Come on, you've earned it. You don't have to drink it all.'

Carly knew she couldn't go on refusing. She reluctantly accepted the glass.

'That's it,' Tom said approvingly.

'Cheers,' said Pippa, raising her glass. 'Here's to a new and better year.'

'Here, here,' agreed Tom.

Tom and Pippa both drank. Carly raised her glass to acknowledge the toast, but didn't drink. She replaced the full glass on the table, staring at it with a morbid fascination. Steven was still enjoying the verbal battle with Tom, although he had no hope of winning.

Carly's hand began to shake as she stared at the glass. It would be so easy to have just one drink. That's all it would take, just one. She lifted the glass once more and held it at eye level, still unable to take her gaze away.

The others hadn't noticed her hesitation and were continuing the happy family bickering. The sound of shattering glass brought their attention back suddenly as Carly dropped the full glass and hurried out of the room.

Tom and Pippa exchanged a puzzled look and, at an imperceptible nod from Pippa, Tom followed Carly quickly.

By the time Tom reached the bedroom, Carly had slammed the door and she ignored Tom's knock. Tom opened the door timidly and poked his head around to see Carly pacing the room tensely.

'Carly...?'

Carly turned to look at him. She couldn't bear to see his kind, loving face. She turned away, very close to tears.

'Hey, what's wrong?' Tom's concern was mirrored in his face.

He crossed the room and put a hand on Carly's shoulder. She turned and almost fell into his arms.

'What is it?'

'I've got to see someone...' Carly began.

'What about? Drugs?'

'No, not drugs...' Once started, Carly couldn't stop.

'Not drugs... God... drinking! Alcohol. I was lying, Tom, 'cos I feel like an alcoholic. I want to stop and I can't. I've tried so hard tonight, but it's just... Oh God, who can I see? I want to get away from all this. You've got to help me...'

Tom was shocked by this outburst. He had, naturally, thought that drugs might be a problem, but drinking? His heart went out to Carly, and he hid his surprise from her as he patted her arm.

He went downstairs, hoping to have a quiet chat with Pippa. Carly had asked for help, and help she would have. Tom couldn't think of anyone who could help, except perhaps Philip. He managed a very quick word with Pippa before the rest of the family interrupted, and then snuck out to make a brief phone call.

When he returned to the living room, Pippa was endeavouring to get Sally to bed.

'I don't want to go to bed,' she protested.

'Yes you do, you look very tired,' replied Tom.

'No I don't.'

'Sal, please... just go to bed. Carly's a bit upset, and the party's over. Okay?'

'Oh, all right,' Sally agreed grumpily, and stalked off to bed.

Just then Bobby entered and called out cheerfully, 'Hi. How is everyone? Hey, Pippa...' She paused as she glanced from one face to the other. Something was wrong. 'What happened?'

'Carly spilt some champagne,' replied Pippa, as she continued to clean up the mess.

'Yeah?' said Bobby lightly. 'Never could hold her grog, could she?'

'Ah, no jokes please.' Tom was alarmed at how close Bobby had inadvertently come to the truth.

Just then, Carly entered the room. Her hair was untidy and she was very pale.

'Ready, love?' asked Tom, and Carly nodded.

'What's going on?' asked Bobby.

'Don't ask me, I just live here,' snapped Steven.

Carly looked at them all. She owed them an explanation. These people had really cared about her, and she owed them that. Whether they would continue to care when they knew the full story didn't bear thinking about.

Steeling herself, she glanced at Tom. 'Have I got a minute? I'd like to explain a few things.' She turned to face the others.

'Do you remember that old T-shirt Frank used to have with the cartoon on it where the guy was saying "No, it can't be, I don't have a drinking problem, I just forgot to stop"? Well, when I was down in the city, I forgot to stop too... and, um... well it's got pretty bad... like it's at the stage now where I want to stop and can't... so I'm trying to do something about it.'

She paused and glanced from one to the other before continuing. 'It isn't going to be easy. But it'll help if no-one makes a big fuss. So, please, if you could just carry on like normal and keep it to yourselves... that'd be great.'

Bobby looked at her feet, unable to meet Carly's gaze. 'Yeah, sure,' she muttered.

'Sure,' said Steven, a little uncertain of how to react to such an admission.

Carly smiled at them all and turned to Tom.

'Let's move, eh?' he said. 'Be back in half an hour or so.'

13

Philip had agreed to meet Tom and Carly at the store, and now the two men were seated while Carly paced the floor, looking tense and edgy.

'How long has it been going on for?' Philip asked.

'Three months or so. From when I left home really,' Carly spoke clearly. She was determined to make this work, and if Philip could help, so much the better.

'Every night?'

Carly nodded. 'Well not at first, but...' She was torn between trying to disguise the problem and realising that honesty was the only way.

'No. I guess it has been every night,' she admitted.

'And it was never just a case of a glass or two after dinner...?'

Tom sat quietly while the conversation continued. His shock was hard to cover, but he knew Carly was doing the right thing, and he trusted Philip.

Carly hesitated at this question, about to answer with a glib lie, then decided to be honest. She shook her head.

'So, once you start, you just keep drinking?'

Carly nodded again. Then, with a dry self-loathing laugh she said, 'Till I went to sleep, anyway. Often I just stayed on the sofa. Then I would wake up and feel terrible. I spent all morning in this haze and never had breakfast. I haven't had breakfast for ages. I can't remember the last time. But after lunch things start to feel better. Then by night-time I feel like a drink again.'

'Do you feel like a drink now?'

Carly looked at Philip sharply. She'd have killed for a drink now, but couldn't bring herself to say it.

'It's not a trap or anything . . .' Philip probed gently.

'Have you got one?' Carly asked, almost eagerly.

'No.'

Carly looked exasperated.

'But you want one, don't you?' Philip persisted.

After a pause, Carly reluctantly nodded.

'And how does that make you feel?'

Carly did not reply, so Philip continued. 'Scared? Angry?'

Carly spun round to face him. 'Yes! Both! All of it!' she exclaimed. 'What does it matter? There's no point in making me feel guilty, for God's sake. I feel guilty as hell already. Can you just tell me what I've done to myself? I just want to get out of this.'

After this emotional outburst, Tom moved to put his arm round her. Seeming to have run out of strength for the moment, she leaned against him. Philip waited for a few minutes, until she had calmed down.

'Well, to state the obvious, you've developed a heavy

84

dependence on alcohol, and lost all self-discipline with regard to intake. So, in that sense, you're addicted.

'But if you're worried about liver damage or brain damage, forget it. It takes years of abuse to wreck your body. Still, that will happen if you don't stop.'

'I'll stop,' said Carly. 'I *want* to stop.'

'Good,' said Philip. 'You've crossed the first bridge then.'

Carly sighed and lifted her head. 'So, what happens now?'

'You go home, you give Tom and Pippa any little supplies you might have hidden somewhere... then you go cold turkey. Clean all the alcohol out of your system. It'll take about seventy-two hours probably... and it'll be seventy-two tough, hard hours.' He turned to Tom and added, 'For you too.'

Tom nodded. What was happening to them? How could Carly have got herself into this state so quickly? He silently thanked the fates that had brought her home, and promised himself that they would do all they could to get her through it.

Philip continued, 'But don't try to use any sort of tranquillisers or sleeping pills to help you through it. That doesn't solve anything. It just creates another dependency. The only way to do this, is to do it cold.'

'And then I'll be right?' asked Carly.

'Ah, no ... not quite. You see, Carly, heavy drinking's just a symptom of something. So, we fix the symptom first, then we have to go looking for the cause.'

'What does that mean?' Carly asked with alarm. 'Not shrinks?'

'Well, counselling. Possibly psychiatry, it depends on the nature of the problem.' Philip was trying to sound reassuring. 'But it's nothing to get uptight about. I fix influenza and they fix alcoholism. There's not much difference really.

'Still, no need to worry about that at this stage,' he went on, realising that the next seventy-two hours would be hard enough for Carly. 'Just go home, and stay strong. In a few days, you'll feel wonderful. I'll drop in tomorrow and see how it's going.'

He smiled at Carly, but her face was a mask. Her immediate future didn't look very bright.

Tom and Carly walked home in silence. Tom draped his arm loosely around her shoulders, and she was glad of the comfort this gave.

They entered the house quietly and didn't encounter anyone as they climbed the stairs. Tom waited while Carly undressed and then gently helped her into bed. Some of the earlier tension was still visible in Carly's manner, but Tom thought she looked okay.

As she reached for the sheets, her hands began to shake. Afraid to look, she clenched her fists tightly and hid her hands under the blankets. Tom stroked the loose hair from her forehead lovingly.

As Tom left the room, he met Pippa in the hallway.

'How is she?' Pippa asked.

Tom shrugged his shoulders.

'What about Bobby?' he asked, realising that Carly would have to have sole occupancy of the bedroom for a while, and wondering where Bobby would sleep.

'Oh, she's okay. Her old van was empty, so she's happy bedding down there.'

'Good,' he replied. 'I think we might have to take shifts staying up tonight.'

Pippa nodded. 'You know, talking to Bobby, I get the impression this hasn't surprised her that much,' she said. 'She didn't say a lot, of course, but I could swear she knew something. How did we miss it, Tom? If the other kids knew, she was obviously drinking when she was still here, so . . .'

'Well, she probably snuck the odd glass, but . . .'

'Why didn't we know?'

'Kids are world champions at hiding things like that. Parents are the last people to find out what's going on.'

Pippa still didn't look very consoled at this.

'This morning,' said Tom, 'you were the one telling me not to go blaming myself.'

He drew Pippa to him and hugged her.

'This isn't happening because of anything we did or didn't do,' he said.

'That's my line,' Pippa responded.

'So take a piece of your own advice. Carly went to the city, she obviously became part of a bad scene, and it's not our job to criticise her or feel responsible. Our job's to help her get over it.'

Pippa considered this for a moment. She looked up

at Tom and nodded. Suddenly, they heard a groan coming from the bedroom.

'Tom . . .!' Carly's voice was tremulous.

Tom turned and started to go in, but Pippa stopped him.

'No. I'll go. You get some sleep,' she said, patting him on the arm, before going in to Carly.

Carly certainly didn't look well. She was shaking quite violently and the perspiration seemed to be pouring from her forehead. She cried out again nervously.

'Tom . . .!'

Pippa hurried to the bedside and wiped a cool handkerchief over Carly's brow.

'Sssh. It's me. It's all right,' she whispered soothingly.

Carly seemed only vaguely aware that Pippa was there, as she fought growing feelings of nausea and disorientation. She lay back in her bed, but seemed unable to settle. Pippa watched with deep concern. It was going to be a long night's journey into day for Carly.

14

A thin strip of light showed from beneath the door of the girls' room. The rest of the house was in darkness, but all was certainly not quiet. Intermittent groans could be heard from behind the bedroom door, followed by short, sharp screams.

The latest scream proved too much for Steven, who had been aware of the disturbance all night. He emerged from his bedroom, pulling on his dressing gown and rubbing his eyes. He hesitated in the hallway, trying to locate the sounds.

As he debated whether to go in to Carly or not, the door to the main bedroom opened and Tom appeared in the hall, not looking much better than Steven.

'Is Pippa in there?' asked Steven.

Tom nodded. 'What time is it?'

'Five after five,' Steven peered at his watch. 'Five o'clock in the morning!' he cried. 'It's been going on all night.'

Just then, another groan seemed to shake the house and there were sounds of vomiting from behind the closed

89

door. Tom hurried into the bedroom. Steven collapsed on the top step and tried to shut out the sounds.

As Tom entered the bedroom, he saw Carly flop back against the pillow as Pippa hastily removed the bowl and wiped her face.

Carly looked dreadful. Her hair was drenched and sticking to her face in matted chunks. Her face was almost grey and her eyes appeared to have sunk into their sockets. She moaned as she tossed her head from side to side.

'How is she?' asked Tom, unnecessarily. He could see that she was in a bad way. He was alarmed to notice that Pippa didn't look much better. She had been up all night, alternately holding the bowl and wiping Carly's forehead and trying, without much success, to calm and comfort the girl.

Carly continued to moan in remorseful delirium. 'How could I do it...? Oh, God... What was...?'

She choked slightly and rose on an elbow. Pippa, sensing that she was going to be sick again, rushed over with the freshly emptied bowl. Carly, however, collapsed back against the pillows.

'Can I get you anything, love?' asked Tom. 'Glass of water, maybe?'

Carly seemed to see through the haze for a second or two. She recognised Tom and Pippa. Pippa reached out to take her hand, but the gesture of affection was too much for Carly to cope with.

Her guilt was so strong that she felt an instinctive reaction to punish herself, to deny herself love and support. She burst into tears and rolled over, unable to face them. She cringed as Tom also tried to put a comforting hand on her shoulder.

Outside the room, the noise had also woken Sally. She joined Steven on the step of the landing.

'You couldn't sleep either, huh?' Steven asked. 'No, don't blame you,' he said as Sally shook her head.

'It sounds really yukky,' said Sally in a small voice. 'She must be dying, is she?'

Steven was thrown by this question. 'What?'

'Carly. Tom said last night she was a bit upset, but she sounds a lot more than a bit upset to me. And I know she went to see the doctor last night, and I know she said something to all of you that I wasn't allowed to hear, so it's got to be something big . . . so I guess she's dying or something.'

'Ah, no. No, Sal, it's not that bad.'

'Well what is it then? And don't you tell me she's just a bit upset, 'cos I'm not thick, you know. I know it's got to be more than that.'

Steven thought about this for a moment. How much should he tell Sally? She was only young, but on the other hand, she lived in the house and was very much aware of what was going on right now. He decided that he should be honest. After all, the poor kid thought Carly was dying.

'Well, yeah, it is more than that,' he said. 'She, um . . . well it's like . . . when she was down in the city, she started drinking a lot. And you know how, when adults drink, they get drunk . . . ?'

91

Sally nodded sagely.

'Well, Carly started getting drunk too, and . . . '

'And this is what happens when you get drunk, is it?' Sally queried.

'Look. Who's telling this story? You or me? Now, this is what happens when you get drunk too often, and hate it, and decide to stop. It's a thing called cold turkey.'

'Cold turkey?' Sally couldn't work that one out at all.

'Yeah. It's a funny name, I know, and it's got a lot to do with drugs and biology and everything, but basically it means you feel sick for two or three days, but then you feel ten times better in the long run.'

Sally absorbed this information slowly and then nodded wisely.

'Oh. So she's not going to die then?'

'Uh, uh,' said Steven, shaking his head. 'She's not going to die, I promise.'

Carly had calmed down a little during the last few minutes. She still looked as though Sally's original assumption could come true at any moment — she looked as if she were dying. She lay still as the painful bout of nausea and disorientation slowly passed.

Pippa picked up the bowl. 'I'll take this out,' she said.

'Then try and get some sleep, all right? I can handle it,' said Tom gently.

Pippa nodded and, with a last glance at Carly, slipped out of the room.

Tom took her place beside the bed. Carly opened her eyes and saw Tom. She quickly closed her eyes and turned her head away. She just couldn't bear to see the hurt look in his eyes. What right had she to their love? She had just caused them pain.

'It's okay. It's okay, love . . .' whispered Tom.

He sat quietly beside her, occasionally stroking her brow and moving the matted hair away from her face. Eventually sleep overcame her, and her breathing steadied. Tom maintained his vigil, anxious that she should not wake alone in the room.

The sun had been up for several hours when Tom was startled by the sound of a car horn outside the house. He frowned at the noise, but was relieved to see that Carly still slept. The first, terrible night was over.

15

In the kitchen, Sally, with the natural resilience of youth, was showing little effect from the almost sleepless night. She sat at the table, amusing herself with her dolls.

'Now you've got to lie there and be sick for seventy-two hours, all right, and then you'll feel a lot better,' she scolded her doll.

Lance and Martin, Summer Bay's inseparable practical jokers, strode in.

'G'day kiddo,' said Martin.

'Hello.'

'What are you doing? Guardin' the house, eh?' Martin had noticed how deserted the house appeared.

'No,' replied Sally, 'just playing. What are you doing?'

'We've got the tape of our new song here. Thought we'd let everyone have a listen,' replied Lance.

'Well, you can't play it now, 'cos Carly's on cold turkey,' said Sally.

'Carly?' said Martin. He could hardly believe his ears.

'Yeah, she came back from the city yesterday and had to have cold turkey,' replied Sally seriously.

Lance's face brightened. 'For brekkie, eh? Yeah, my mum used to do that too.'

To say that Martin was marginally brighter than Lance was not paying him any real compliment. The two could invariably be found together, Martin feeding off Lance's hero worship. However, this comment from Lance astounded even Martin.

He had immediately grasped the implications of 'cold turkey' and proceeded to pump Sally for more information. Sally quickly lost interest in the two boys and, apart from telling Martin that Carly had been sick all night, didn't enlighten them any further.

'Come on, mate,' Martin said to Lance. 'Let's go.'

Lance was totally mystified by the sudden turn of events. They had come over to play their new song, and now Martin was dashing out as if he had just won the lottery and couldn't wait to spend it.

A few minutes later, the two boys were seated at a table in a quiet corner of Ailsa's coffee shop. Martin had slowly and painfully explained to Lance the implications of Sally's remarks.

'*That* cold turkey!' cried Lance, the light dawning.

'Yeah, you drongo. The drug sort, not the food sort.'

They discussed the possibilities for a few minutes.

'Yeah, bummer, eh?' Lance was saying. 'Imagine what people like Celia Stewart and Betty Falwell are gonna say about that. You'd think they woulda tried to keep it under wraps, wouldn't ya?'

Suddenly Martin slapped Lance on the back.

'Oh, hell,' he said. 'We only heard it from Sal. What

96

if she just overheard it or something? Maybe she's off gabbin' it to everyone while Tom and Pippa think it's still a secret. You don't see anyone in here talkin' about it, do you?' Lance nodded uncertainly.

'Let's get back there,' said Martin, as he leapt up and headed for the door, followed by a faithful, if somewhat confused, Lance.

The two boys rushed back to the Fletcher house and confronted Tom as soon as they burst through the door. Without giving too much away, Tom tried to establish exactly what the two knew.

'Who did Sally hear it from?' he asked.

Martin was spokesman for the two. 'We don't know. All we know is what she told us, which is why we thought it must be drugs.'

'I mean, we don't want to get Sal in trouble, but we just thought maybe she wasn't s'posed to know. She might go round tellin' people . . .'

Tom paused for a moment. He was anxious to find Sally, who seemed to have disappeared, but he realised that the boys already knew half the truth.

'Look, Carly's problem is alcohol, not drugs,' he explained. 'But she is going through hell. She can't even face me and Pippa, for heaven's sake, let alone a town full of gloating gossip-mongers! Particularly if they get the story wrong and think she's a drug addict. God, I don't know how she'd cope with that.'

'We'd better find Sal, then, before she tells anyone else, eh?' said Martin, heading for the door.

'Yeah,' agreed Tom. 'I'll just tell Pip where I'm off to, then we'll get cracking.'

Unfortunately, Sally had already been out and about.

Alison was lazing on the beach, only just tolerating her younger sister, who was building sandcastles and imploring Alison to help.

'I don't want to help you build a sandcastle,' said Alison. 'Why don't you get one of your friends to help you?'

'Because they all had to go, that's why. Janet had to go because her mum said so, and Sally was too tired 'cos her sister Carly was sick all night and kept her awake.'

Alison was instantly alert.

'She was sick?' she asked.

'Yeah, she was throwing up cold turkey all night or something; it sounded gross.'

Alison could hardly believe her ears.

'*What* was she doing?'

'She said she'd been having cold turkey all night and it was making her throw up and everything, but she had to have it to get better. Now will you help me with the sandcastle?'

But there was no answer from her sister. Alison wasn't listening. So *that's* why Carly came back!

A short time later, Alison was holding court in Ailsa's

coffee shop. Surrounded by several of her cronies, she was expounding on the gossip she had picked up.

'She's a junkie, that's why she had to come back. My kid sister found out from her kid sister. I don't know what drug she was on, but knowing what a write-off she is, it was probably something really heavy. I mean, what a degenerate.'

Standing by the counter, Ailsa had not been listening, but towards the end of this, the general meaning started to sink in, and she was instantly alert.

'But then it's not a huge surprise, is it? When you think how she was kicked out of her own family when she was still a kid and then taken up by the Fletchers of all people ... well, really ... what chance have you got? And you know what they say, don't you? Once an addict, always an addict.'

Ailsa called Alison over, furious with what she had heard.

'If you say one more word about Carly Morris, you can get out of the shop,' she warned.

'Oooh, we are touchy, aren't we? Hit a nerve, have I?'

Turning to her friends, Alison continued, 'I bet Bobby Simpson's the Summer Bay connection. Explains how she got the money to buy into this place, doesn't it?'

The group sniggered at this, but Alison's smile froze on her face as Ailsa grabbed her and manhandled her out of the door. She landed with a heavy thump and had difficulty rising with any dignity in front of her friends. She cast one triumphant smile at Ailsa before the door slammed in her face.

16

It was mid-morning before Carly stirred. She woke fitfully, tossing her head and gradually realising that the sun was streaming in through the window. Her face showed ample evidence of the night before. Her skin had taken on a grey, almost translucent look and there were deep circles under her bloodshot eyes. She struggled to sit up.

Pulling on her dressing gown, she moved across to the window, suddenly in need of fresh air. As she tried to open the window, she noticed that her hands were shaking violently. The effort of opening the window was almost too much for her, and she realised how weak she was. With a deep sigh, she managed to throw it open and breathed the fresh air eagerly.

A light tap on the door brought her attention back, but she didn't move. Bobby poked her head in.

'Can I come in? How're you feelin'?'

Carly turned to look at Bobby with a wry frown. 'How do I look?' she asked.

Bobby looked and realised that the question did not

require an answer. If Carly felt half as bad as that, she didn't want to talk about it.

'I gotta say, I'm pretty impressed, Carls,' she went on. 'It took a lot of guts to admit you were screwin' up, and what you're havin' to go through now . . . gees, I don't know, it must be hell. I really admire you for doin' it.'

Carly smiled her thanks to Bobby for this and turned as she heard a car pull up outside. She was relieved to notice that it was only Philip, but suddenly a thought struck her. What if Philip had told anyone? What if everyone knew?

Bobby recognised a note of paranoia in Carly's voice and reassured her that there was nothing unnatural about Philip visiting them. There was no way that he would tell anyone.

'Calm down, okay?' she said. 'Everything's cool. You're doin' great.'

Downstairs, however, Pippa was explaining to Philip that everything was *not* cool. She was hastily outlining the fact that Sally had told at least Martin and Lance about the cold turkey. Sally had sworn that she had told no-one else, and they hoped that the gossip would end there.

Philip examined Carly and reported to Pippa that she was coming along as expected. He warned them that last night's symptoms would return; they weren't out of the woods yet.

Carly had been pleased to see Philip. His professional understanding was more acceptable to

102

her at the moment than the love and care which flowed from Pippa and Tom. Although she knew that she couldn't do this without them, Carly still felt so badly about the way she had treated them that she found it hard to face that love.

She stood at the window and watched as Philip's car moved off down the driveway. She was about to turn away from the window when a voice from below made her stop. It was Donald Fisher.

'Mrs Fletcher...'

Pippa opened the door and Fisher climbed the steps of the verandah so that Carly could no longer see him. They stood at the door talking, so the voices drifted up to her quite clearly.

'I'm glad I've caught you in,' Fisher said. 'I was wondering if you have time for a chat. It is rather important.'

'What's it about?' Pippa enquired cautiously.

'It's about Carly actually. Or more specifically about Carly's request to repeat Year Twelve. I feel it may be difficult to honour my acceptance of this request if there is any substance to the rumours which are presently sweeping through town.'

Pippa's heart sank. 'Rumours?' she asked.

Carly listened with mounting horror as Fisher went on.

'Yes, one hears she is a drug addict.'

'What!' Pippa's surprise was genuine; she hadn't expected that.

'I don't know where it originated, but everyone's

saying it, and everyone seems to believe it, so I can only assume there is at least some element of truth in it. And naturally, if this is the case . . .'

'But it *isn't* the case!' cried Pippa.

'I can hardly enrol someone with a known history of drug abuse,' Fisher went on self-righteously.

Pippa suddenly realised that their voices were raised. 'Donald, will you please keep your voice down. She does *not* have a history of drug abuse, and she isn't an addict. It's all lies.'

'You can guarantee that, can you? There is absolutely no credence to be placed in these stories whatsoever?'

This caused Pippa to hesitate. She couldn't lie.

'No. Well, not as they are. It definitely has nothing to do with drugs, I can positively guarantee that. Come inside for a minute. I'll just go and have a word with Carly. Whether you have to know or not, I won't say anything unless she wants me to.'

Pippa left Fisher and made her way upstairs. She tapped on the bedroom door and poked her head inside.

'Carly?'

There was no answer, and Pippa's eyes went immediately to the open window. The room was empty and, as she realised that Carly must have heard the whole conversation, she slumped against the doorway and groaned.

At Celia's store, the flames of gossip were being

anned. Celia was enjoying herself thoroughly as she
illed Betty Falwell in on the latest news in Summer
Bay. They had a drug addict in their midst.

'If I were the Fletchers,' Betty was saying. 'I wouldn't
be taking her back... they're too soft for their own
good, and they won't be told.'

'I know,' agreed Celia. 'That girl's always been wild,
but they wouldn't hear a word against her. I always
knew Carly would come to a bad end.'

The words were barely out of her mouth when Carly
herself burst into the shop and rushed over to Celia.

The detoxification process was taking its toll. One
minute she was sweating profusely, the next she was
shivering. She was wearing an odd assortment of
clothes, the first things that had come to hand in her
haste to leave the house. Her desperation was making
her slightly manic, but she was too out of touch with
reality to be aware of the impression she was making.
Betty and Celia looked at her in shock.

'You have to help me, Celia,' gasped Carly. 'You've
got to tell everyone I'm not on drugs. I know, I look
like a junkie, but that's because I'm detoxing! That's
what you tell people, right? I'm a boozer, not a junkie!
You must tell them! Please!'

For once, neither Betty nor Celia said anything, they
just stared at Carly in amazement.

Back at the house, frantic phone calls were not helping
to locate Carly. Bobby was in the coffee shop, thinking

that Carly might have gone there. She was following Matt around as he wiped the tables, trying to get him to understand the urgency of the situation.

'If Carly shows up, call Pippa, okay?'

'What if she won't stay?' remarked Matt indifferently.

'Lock the door,' exclaimed Bobby.

'Great! Locked up with a manic depressive!'

'You're a big help.'

'I've had it with her!'

Matt was stopped from saying anything further by the sight of Carly rushing in. Ignoring Bobby altogether, she spoke to Matt with desperation in her voice.

'We have to talk.'

Matt turned to Bobby, saying, 'Take her home, wil ya?'

'Please,' Carly was almost hysterical.

'If she wants to talk, you listen,' snapped Bobby angrily. 'I'm gonna shut Alison Patterson up.'

With that, she strode out of the coffee shop, leaving Matt with a trapped expression on his face.

Realising he couldn't avoid the conversation, Matt sat down with Carly, but he was coldly offhand refusing to let her reach him again.

'There's no excuse for the way I've treated you ... bu I'm the one who came off second best,' Carly began.

'So we're quits.'

'Don't shut me out, Matt. I know I've been the pits but ...'

'But you won't do it again...' Matt finished the sentence for her.

'I mean it this time.'

'You always say that, too.'

'Matt...please!'

Matt rose from the table and turned to continue with his work. Carly stood up quickly and, as she went to put a hand on his arm to stop him, her knees buckled and she would have fallen had Matt not caught her. He carefully sat her on a stool.

'You should've stayed in bed,' he said.

'I wanted you to know that I wasn't on drugs.'

'What you do with your life is none of my business any more.' Despite the cold words, Matt's voice was showing signs of softening. 'Hang in there... you'll make it.'

He fetched a glass of water for Carly, and she suddenly realised that Matt was feeling sorry for her. In a moment of clarity, she saw a way that she could use this to get him back on side.

'I'm scared, Matt,' she said. 'I don't think I can do this by myself.'

Matt tried to withstand the emotional blackmail, but in the end he relented.

'You won't have to. I'll be there,' he said reassuringly.

He wrapped his jacket around her shivering shoulders and gently led her home.

As they entered the Fletcher house Pippa met them at

the doorway. Matt was supporting an obviously sick and weak Carly.

'Take it easy,' he whispered to her.

Carly clutched his jacket around her.

'Thanks,' said Pippa to Matt. 'I'll take it from here.' She turned to Carly. 'Give Matt his jacket.'

The jacket was a security blanket for Carly, and she wouldn't give it up. She didn't want to let Matt go yet either.

'Bobby'll mind the shop. Won't you stay and talk to me for a while? Please...'

Pippa sensed Matt's reluctance to stay as he gave in and agreed. She exchanged a knowing look with him as he led Carly upstairs. Pippa's expression was still registering concern when Philip entered the house, carrying his medical bag.

'Oh, Philip... I'm glad Bobby caught up with you.'

'She said Carly was in a bad way.'

'She's got the shakes again.'

Philip moved to go upstairs. 'I'll check her out,' he said.

'Matt's with her at the moment,' said Pippa.

Philip stopped for a moment. 'I thought that was all over?' he said in surprise.

'Carly does a nice line in emotional blackmail. And Matt's a pushover for a sob story,' said Pippa frankly.

'All she's doing is replacing alcohol with another emotional crutch,' said Philip.

Pippa felt a flash of annoyance at what she saw as Philip's intolerant attitude.

108

'She *needs something* to get through that seventy-two hours!' she snapped.

Philip remained calm. 'Of course she does,' he said. 'Love and understanding from her family. Not lies from a reluctant boyfriend.'

Pippa realised that there was a lot of truth in what Philip said.

'What should I tell Matt then, Philip?' she asked.

'If he wants to see her through the detox, fine. But after that, he has to be honest with her,' replied Philip.

'Couldn't he leave it for a while?'

'Sure. But when he walks out on her, she'll get straight back on the bottle.'

'And have to go through all this withdrawal again? No way!' Pippa couldn't conceive of anyone willingly going through that.

'Neurotics don't think like that,' Philip said. 'Carly drinks because it destroys short-term memory. So anything she doesn't want to face gets blotted out.'

Pippa nodded. 'I'll tell Matt he's off the hook.'

When Matt reappeared, Pippa was busy in the kitchen.

'How's it going?' she called to Matt over her shoulder.

'She's dozed off,' he replied.

They chatted for a few minutes, then Matt headed for the door.

'See ya, Mrs Fletcher.'

'Matt,' Pippa sounded hesitant. 'Will you be back?'

'Oh... yeah,' said Matt, tensely.

'But you wish you could duck it?'

'I did try to be straight with her. But you know what Carly's like when she wants something.'

'Whatever it takes, she'll do it,' agreed Pippa.

'That makes her sound worse than she is. She's got a lot going for her, but . . .' Matt couldn't seem to find the words.

'The good side of her nature is always fighting a losing battle with the bad side,' Pippa finished for him.

'Yeah,' he agreed. 'I always seem to be around when the bad side's winning.'

'Join the club.'

'How do you hack it?'

'You love people despite their faults . . . sometimes because of them,' Pippa sighed.

'She's lucky to have you,' said Matt.

'I wouldn't swap her for quids either. But I don't expect you to feel the same. So if you want to go out that door and keep going . . .'

'When I make a promise, I keep it,' declared Matt loyally. 'I want to see her through the bad stuff. If you think it'll help.'

'It'll help a lot,' Pippa said. 'But once she's dried out, you have to tell her it's over.'

'Every time I try, she just tunes me out.'

'Maybe actions speak louder than words . . .' Pippa said knowingly.

Matt regarded her for a moment, then realisation struck him.

'Yeah . . .' he said with a smile.

110

17

Celia and Betty were only too happy to comply with Carly's wishes. They loved a good story, especially when it had come straight from the horse's mouth. They were seated at a table in the sun, outside Celia's store, having a cup of coffee and ensuring that no-one passed without hearing the news.

'If Pippa Fletcher says it's the drink, you can take it as gospel,' Celia was saying to a departing shopper. 'So do spread the word, and if I hear anything more, you'll be the first to know. 'Bye.'

Alison was sitting at a nearby table, toying with a milkshake. Celia was certainly doing a good job of spreading the word. Alison had been thrilled to think that Carly was on drugs and didn't want to give up on the story too quickly.

As she sat brooding, Bobby burst out of the shop, brandishing a book.

'Listen to this!' she cried, heading for Alison's table.

'Where did you get that?' asked Celia, shocked. 'Who told you you could help yourself to Philip's property?'

'I'm only borrowing it. It's all about alcohol withdrawal. The symptoms are vomiting, disorientation, shakes, sweating, short-term memory loss... and Carly's got the lot. Not drugs — booze,' she glared triumphantly at Alison.

'Yes,' said Celia. 'Pippa cleared up the misunderstanding.'

'And the family that tells lies together, stays together,' snarled Alison.

Bobby glared at her and slammed the book shut.

'Alcohol withdrawal — yeah, sure! Everyone knows it takes years to get hooked on booze. But you can become a junkie like that,' said Alison, snapping her fingers.

'I don't blame you for being sceptical, Alison. I was too, till Pippa Fletcher set me straight,' said Celia.

'And telling you anything's as good as taking out a full-page ad, isn't it?' Alison taunted. 'Well, I'm going to spread the word about the dreadful milkshakes you sell here. And about Carly Morris. You can't kid me she's not a junkie.'

With that, she stormed off, leaving Celia and Betty looking on disapprovingly.

'That girl is insufferable. Like talking to a brick wall!' remarked Celia.

A little later that day, Alison was stretched out on the beach soaking up the sun. She jumped violently as a hand suddenly latched onto her foot and someone started dragging her into the water.

112

Bobby was so angry that she didn't stop until she had dragged the struggling Alison into the water. She held Alison's head under the water for several seconds before allowing her to surface, spluttering.

'Is Carly an alkie or a druggie?' Bobby demanded.

'Druggie.' Alison was still defiant.

Bobby pushed her head under again.

'Try to get it right this time,' said Bobby coldly.

Alison was still determined, but she was smart enough to know when she was in a no-win situation.

'Alkie,' she muttered.

'Didn't hear that.'

'Alkie.'

'Right,' said Bobby, releasing Alison. 'And if I hear you've been saying she's a junkie, it'll never be safe for you to go in the water again.'

Carly was going through another bad spell. As she emerged from the bathroom, Pippa was waiting anxiously for her.

'You okay?' she enquired.

'No,' replied Carly, only too glad of Pippa's support as they limped into the living room.

'Some water?' Pippa asked anxiously.

'Couldn't keep it down,' Carly said as she sat down.

'Why don't you go back up to bed?'

'I might have to make another dash in a minute.'

'I'll get a bowl,' said Pippa, but Carly shook her head.

'You don't have to crack hardy,' Pippa tried to soothe her. 'This is a team effort.'

'Thanks,' said Carly, taking her head in her hands and groaning. 'The jackhammers are starting up again.'

She relented and allowed Pippa to lead her upstairs and put her to bed.

'I've only felt like this once before... when I had food poisoning, but they could treat that,' she moaned.

'I know it's rough, but you've come a long way.'

'You don't have to give me the pep talk. I promised Matt I'd make it, and I will.'

Pippa tried not to react to this remark, but Carly went on, 'He's so good for me Pippa... so safe and dependable... I can tell you exactly what he's doing right now.'

A misty look came over her face as she visualised Matt. He would be at the beach, surfing, she knew. Then he would come to see her and they would talk about all the things they would do together when she was better.

Matt was not, in fact, at the beach at that moment, but was perched on the edge of a desk in the Macklin Development Company office talking to Ruth Stewart.

'She just won't let go, and it's really getting to me,' he was saying to Roo. 'That's why I'm here. I need a favour.'

114

Roo regarded him warily.

'I want you to pretend we're dating,' Matt explained his plan.

'No way, Jose!' was Roo's instinctive reaction. 'You don't kick someone when they're down.'

'So you think I should get her hopes up and then put in the boot?'

'When's our first date?' asked Roo resignedly.

'How about tonight?' Matt was considerably cheered.

'I've got something else on,' said Roo. 'I'm going to the drive-in with Martin.'

'Martin Dibble?' exclaimed Matt.

'He's really nice when you get to know him. And he was a friend to me when I needed one.'

'Maybe I should tag along to protect you, I hear he's an octopus,' said Matt.

'I won't need it, we're just good friends, but come anyway.'

'You sure he won't mind?'

'You know Martin ... two's company, three's a party,' replied Roo.

As far as Roo was concerned, she and Martin might be just good friends, but that evening at the drive-in it was obvious that Martin didn't share these sentiments.

The expression on Martin's face left no doubt that he was feeling the odd man out as they sat, all three, in the front seat of Martin's car.

Roo was seated between the two boys and was happily chatting to Matt about various movies they had both seen. Martin couldn't even concentrate on the movie, as the pair whispered and laughed at what were seemingly private jokes.

At interval, Roo went to the rest rooms and Matt volunteered to go for ice-creams. Alone in the car, Martin fumed. How dare that Matt character cut in on his territory? He had been trying to win Roo for ages now. She wasn't just the sort of girl you picked up at a party. He had been sending her flowers and asking her out for weeks, until she had finally accepted. Then she had to bring along this jerk.

His anger finally getting the better of him, Martin locked all the doors of the car. When Matt returned, ice-creams dripping down his hands, he knocked on the window.

'Rack off,' said Martin angrily, winding the window down a few centimetres. 'Roo's my date, so butt out.'

'Look,' hissed Matt, trying not to let everyone in the drive-in know what was going on, as he tried to talk to Martin through the crack in the window. 'There's no need to get aggro... I'm not trying to crack onto her...'

'Sure you're not. And you're not cheating on Carly,' growled Martin.

'That's over.'

'Then how come you brought her home today?'

'I felt sorry for her.'

'You must think I'm an idiot.'

Matt bit back the obvious comment.

'Carly's off the air, right?' Martin went on. 'So what do you do for action? You give Roo a sob story so you're back in business till Carly's up to it again.'

'I don't want Carly back,' Matt explained in exasperation. 'That's why Roo's pretending to date me. It's the only way to get the message across. If you don't believe me, open the back door and I'll just sit in the back.'

Unfortunately for Martin, Roo arrived back just as the lights dimmed and the second half of the movie began. She immediately hopped into the back seat, next to Matt.

'How's that for timing?' she said, quite oblivious to the fact that Martin was now left alone in the front seat.

Matt looked helplessly at Martin as he reached forward to give him his rapidly melting ice-cream. The choc-top fell out of the cone and landed in a squishy mess in Martin's lap. It was definitely not Martin's night.

18

Carly was leading Philip to the bedroom door. He had finished his examination and was satisfied that the detoxification process was going according to plan. Carly looked drawn and haggard, but she was not shaking and her face was determined.

'You're doing well,' said Philip.

'I'll make it,' Carly said with a weak smile. 'I've got to, for Matt's sake. He's fantastic. Been here as often as he could ... just sitting with me, holding my hand. It's been really gross at times, but he stayed with me.'

'Good for him,' Philip remarked with more conviction than he felt. 'It's obviously helped you through the worst part. But you have to realise that it's not over yet. This isn't the end of it; it's the beginning, I'm afraid. You'll have to be just as strong, if not stronger, in the weeks to come. Okay?'

'I'll be all right,' nodded Carly. 'I've got to be, for Matt. Now we're back together again, I can get through anything.'

Philip smiled at her reassuringly, but inside he had grave doubts. He must speak to Matt.

The next morning, he found Matt at the beach. Philip was waiting on the sand as Matt emerged from the surf, dripping with water, bronzed and fit.

'G'day,' said Philip.

'Hi, Phil. Good surf.'

'I haven't got time to catch waves, worse luck. I came down to see you about Carly.'

'She okay?' Matt sounded anxious.

'She will be. I hear she's been leaning on you quite a bit?'

'Yeah ... well, she reckoned she needed me around, if she was gonna kick the drinking,' Matt sounded embarrassed.

'Look, mate,' Philip said. 'It's terrific of you to want to help her like that, but you're not really doing her any favours. She's got to stand on her own two feet, and she shouldn't use emotional blackmail on you to keep you with her all the time.'

'I was gonna tell her ...' Matt stammered.

Philip nodded. 'Make it sooner, rather than later.'

'I thought it might make it easier for her, if I was going out with someone else,' Matt explained. 'It wouldn't be like I was rejecting her, just for herself, you know what I mean?'

Philip shrugged. 'It might help,' he said. 'Either way, she's got to face up to her problems, without relying on alcohol, or you, or anything else.'

'Yeah, s'pose you're right...' said Matt, looking down.

Matt sat on the sand for a long time after Philip had left. He couldn't shake the dreadful feeling that he was somehow going to hurt Carly. He knew, though, that there could never be anything between them again, and what Philip said made sense. Eventually, he shrugged his shoulders and, grabbing his board, made for the surf again.

The next morning, a very determined Matt greeted Pippa briefly as he strode through the house. Pippa watched him climb the stairs to Carly's room, knowing that something was not right.

'I'm so glad you're here,' exclaimed Carly when he knocked and went into the room. 'Come and give me a cuddle.'

Matt reluctantly approached her and sat down beside her. He was torn with guilt at the purpose of his visit, but determined to get it over.

'Carly,' he began. 'I came to see you 'cos I have to tell you something. I wanted to stick with you while you were going through all the sickness and that, but... as far as you and me going out together... well... I'm sorry, it's just not going to work.'

This was too devastating a notion for Carly to take seriously.

'Yes it is!' she cried, feverishly.

Matt was firm. 'No it's not.'

Carly started to panic. Tears welled in her eyes as she pleaded with him.

'Matt, please don't do this. If you're not around, I'll go back on the grog, I know I will. I won't be able to stop myself,' she cried, resorting to the same tactics that had worked before.

Matt's face showed none of the emotion that was churning inside him as he rose and turned at the door.

'Yes you will,' he said firmly. 'I've talked to Philip, and he says you have to get over this by yourself. Look, I like you, and I care about you, but I've got another girlfriend now, and it's just all over between us, okay?'

He strode from the room, Carly's pleas and sobs echoing in his ears.

Pippa and Tom spent an anxious day. Carly locked her door and wouldn't answer any of their calls. They could hear heartbroken sobbing issuing from the room, but she wouldn't come out, even for lunch.

By tea time, however, she came downstairs. The conversation was monosyllabic on Carly's part, despite the family's efforts to chat about unimportant things. As soon as the meal was over, Carly retreated to her room.

Oh Lord, thought Pippa. What's happening? How will she cope with this?

19

It was a bright, summer morning as Bobby burst into the house through the back door, with Sally in hot pursuit. Bobby was clutching a large box and her eyes were shining.

'Please can I see it?' begged Sally. 'I promise I won't tell anyone what it's like.'

'No. N–O.' said Bobby.

'I bet you're going to let Carly see it.'

'She's me bridesmaid . . . and me room-mate.'

'She stays there all the time,' said Sally grumpily.

'You mean she hasn't surfaced yet?' Bobby sounded surprised.

As if on cue, Carly came into the room, still in her dressing gown and carrying nail polish and a magazine.

'I've got the wedding dress,' Bobby said excitedly. 'Wanna see it?'

She finally managed to evict a protesting Sally from the room and returned to find Carly, seemingly disinterested, painting her nails.

'I thought you weren't gonna spend the rest of your life sittin' round mopin' about Matt,' she said.

'I'm not,' protested Carly.

'Nah...' Bobby was scornful. 'You always put on hot pink nail polish before breakfast.'

'Look,' flared Carly. 'What do you expect! It wasn't easy going through all that detox stuff... and then finding out the person you thought cared about you, didn't.'

'You can't keep leanin' on him, Carly,' Bobby said gently.

'All right,' said Carly, putting on a show of confidence. 'Let's see the dress.'

With a flourish, Bobby produced the dress. It was absolutely beautiful. It had been Pippa's wedding dress, and they had had it altered to suit Bobby perfectly.

'Whaddya reckon?' she asked, her eyes shining.

'Not bad.'

'"Not bad"?' she cried. 'It's ace. Pippa told the woman how we wanted it, and she's done it exactly right.'

'I think I should pull out,' said Carly.

'What of? The wedding? You're s'posed to be me main bridesmaid.'

Carly looked at Bobby. The shining eyes had given way to a look of desperation as Bobby fought to control herself. She not only wanted Carly as bridesmaid desperately, she felt it would be the best thing for her. It would help get her mind off Matt and the grog.

'Everyone knows all the hassles I've been having,' Carly mumbled. 'It'll spoil it for you.'

In fact, she was terrified at the prospect of following Bobby down the aisle, with the whole town watching.

'Oh sure,' said Bobby scathingly. 'They'll all be looking at you. No-one would be interested in me. The town derro... the kid with about as many prospects as the hunchback of Notre Dame... marryin' the best lookin' guy in Summer Bay... Who'd even give me a second glance when Carly Morris is there to stare at, eh?'

Carly held her gaze for a moment, then the logic of what Bobby had said hit her.

'All right... I'll do it,' she agreed.

Bobby bounced out of the house with her precious box under her arm. Nothing was going to spoil her wedding day.

The house was strangely quiet when Bobby returned an hour or so later. As she entered the kitchen, her eye fell immediately on a bottle of brandy sitting squarely in the middle of the table.

Bobby paused for a second, taking in the whole scene at a glance. Carly was sitting at the table, her eyes fixed on the two-thirds-full bottle. She glanced at her watch and then went back to what appeared to be a vigil.

'What!' cried Bobby. 'Are you crazy?'

'No,' said Carly, frustrated. 'You've got the wrong idea...'

Bobby reached over and snatched the bottle from the table, but Carly angrily grabbed it back.

'I just wanted to prove a point,' she said. 'That I could be in the same room as a bottle of alcohol and not drink it.'

'Oh, yeah,' said Bobby sceptically. 'How long did it take you to think of that one?'

'It isn't an excuse. I haven't even got a glass out. I'm telling the truth.'

Her earnest explanation began to sound quite genuine to Bobby.

'All right,' she said. 'Now you've looked at it, I'll put it away.'

'No,' Carly said firmly, stopping Bobby from taking the bottle. 'I haven't finished timing it yet. I gave myself ten minutes. There're still seven to go.'

'Fine,' shrugged Bobby. 'Don't mind me.'

'Alone,' Carly said pointedly.

Bobby was still worried. 'What if you don't make it?'

'I will,' said Carly firmly.

Finally, Bobby relented and left the room, whereupon Carly resumed her vigil, glancing at her watch from time to time.

Bobby could contain herself no longer. About fifteen minutes later, she burst back into the kitchen.

The bottle was still in the middle of the table, but it was empty and Carly was nowhere to be seen.

She swung angrily to face Carly as she appeared from the pantry.

'Hi,' said Carly brightly.

'So much for willpower,' Bobby spat at her.

Carly knew exactly what she meant, but said casually, 'Oh, that... Some of us can hold it better than others I guess.'

Bobby looked completely outraged as Carly grinned. From behind her back she produced a carton of orange juice.

'Pretty strong stuff, orange juice,' she said.

'Don't look so disgusted. I didn't drink it. I tipped it all down the sink,' she said proudly.

Bobby was secretly impressed, but not prepared to show Carly how she felt. They bickered for a while, about nothing in particular, until they both realised how silly they were being.

'Sorry to hassle you just before the wedding,' apologised Carly.

'Listen,' said Bobby. 'How about we burn off the aggro? Hit the town? You know, a hen's night. Pick up Narelle and go ragin'... celebrate me last night of freedom. Whaddya reckon?'

'Great,' said Carly, until realisation struck her. 'Except for one thing.'

'We don't have to drink to enjoy ourselves,' assured Bobby.

'Yeah, but in the city... raging...?'

'You're cured, aren't ya?'

'I don't trust myself... not yet.'

'No, Narelle and me'll slap your wrist if you start gettin' pangs. You in, or not?'

'Why not!' Carly agreed.

Hasty phone calls followed, and arrangements were made. Mid-afternoon saw the two girls bounding out of the Fletcher house towards Tom's car. Carly looked better than she had in days. She had dressed carefully and had applied a flattering make-up.

'You sure Tom doesn't mind us taking the car?' Carly asked.

'No sweat. Long as we stay over at Narelle's and get back early tomorra mornin',' replied Bobby cheerfully.

'Where are you going?' Sally asked

'To the city . . . for some heavy ragin',' said Bobby.

'What do you do when you rage?'

'See a band . . .' Bobby told her.

'Have a few drinks . . .' added Carly.

Bobby shot a questioning look at Carly.

'Cappuccinos,' Carly added with a smile.

They gaily hopped into the car and, a few minutes later, all Sally could see was a rapidly disappearing cloud of dust.

20

The morning of the wedding dawned bright and clear. The two girls were as good as their word; they had returned early and were now in the living area behind the store, regaling Frank with stories of their night.

'It was great,' said Carly. 'Specially what we did after the band.'

Carly and Bobby exchanged knowing looks.

'Like what?' asked Frank suspiciously.

Carly grinned at Bobby. 'Think we should tell him?'

'Dunno if he's old enough,' laughed Bobby.

'Give up!' cried Frank. 'Just tell me, will you?'

'We went to a male strip joint,' said Bobby.

'You're joking!!' Frank exclaimed.

'It was a laugh a minute. All these really horrible guys gyratin' round like they were sexy or somethin',' Bobby told him.

'Narelle gave them heaps,' added Carly.

'Reckons they all oughta enter the Mr Puniverse competition.'

'That's when we got kicked out... for being too noisy,' said Carly, obviously enjoying herself.

Frank smiled at them. 'Sounds like a wild night.'

'Why should the blokes have all the fun?' asked Bobby. 'Carly didn't touch a drop, either.'

'Reckon I could get to like mineral water,' said Carly wryly.

She and Bobby exchanged glances and gave each other the thumbs up.

Feeling then that she was imposing on the two lovebirds on their wedding day, Carly headed off for the house to begin preparations for the big event.

As she walked along, she realised that she felt better than she had for months. She had been unsure about the girls' night out in the city, but now she knew if she could lick that, and still have a good time, she would be right.

She was excited now at the thought of the wedding. It would be a great day for Bobby and Frank, and her chance to show Summer Bay that she was back in the human race. She still had to face the prospect of returning to school, and she knew that she would be in for some stirring there. Still, she consoled herself, it'd be a nine-day wonder and they'd soon lose interest in her.

The memory of Matt still ached inside her, but she had to ask herself whether she had really loved him or whether she had just wanted him because she sensed she couldn't have him this time. Also, she had needed someone to lean on, but she would be all right now.

130

She had agreed with Philip to attend counselling sessions because, as he pointed out, there was still a long road to hoe. Somehow, though, Carly knew she would make it.

Stevie Day
Series
JACQUELINE WILSON

Supersleuth	£2.25	☐
Lonely Hearts	£2.25	☐
Rat Race	£2.25	☐
Vampire	£2.25	☐

An original new series featuring an unlikely but irresistible heroine – fourteen-year-old Stevie Day, a small skinny feminist who has a good eye for detail which, combined with a wild imagination, helps her solve mysteries.

"Jacqueline Wilson is a skilful writer, readers of ten and over will find the (Stevie Day) books good, light-hearted entertainment."

Children's Books December 1987

"Sparky Stevie" *T.E.S. January 1988*

ARMADA

Eunice Gottlieb

TRICIA SPRINGSTUBB

This hilarious new series features the irresistible Eunice Gottlieb who spends her time dreaming of breaking away from the chaos of her family. Contemporary, fast-paced and very incisive, these adventures make compulsive reading.

ARMADA

Run With the Hare

LINDA NEWBERY

A sensitive and authentic novel exploring the workings of an animal rights group, through the eyes of Elaine, a sixth-form pupil. Elaine becomes involved with the group through her more forceful friend Kate, and soon becomes involved with Mark, an Adult Education student and one of the more sophisticated members of the group. Elaine finds herself painting slogans and sabotaging a fox hunt. Then she and her friends uncover a dog fighting ring – and things turn very nasty.

£1.95 □

Hairline Cracks

JOHN ROBERT TAYLOR

A gritty, tense and fast-paced story of kidnapping, fraud and cover ups. Sam Lydney's mother knows too much. She's realized that a public inquiry into the safety of a nuclear power station has been rigged. Now she's disappeared and Sam's sure she has been kidnapped, he can trust no one except his resourceful friend Mo, and together they are determined to uncover the crooks' operation and, more importantly, find Sam's mother.

£1.95 □

ARMADA

Have you seen
the Hardy Boys
lately?

Now you can continue to enjoy the Hardy Boys in a new action-packed series written especially for older readers. Each book has more high-tech adventure, intrigue, mystery and danger than ever before.

Join Frank and Joe in these fabulous adventures, available only in Armada.

1	Dead on Target	£2.25	☐
2	Evil, Incorporated	£2.25	☐
3	Cult of Crime	£2.25	☐
4	The Lazarus Plot	£2.25	☐

ARMADA

The Chalet School
Series
ELINOR M. BRENT-DYER

Elinor M. Brent-Dyer has written many books about life at the famous alpine school. Follow the thrilling adventures of Joey, Mary-Lou and all the other well-loved characters in these delightful stories, available only in Armada.

ARMADA

Have you seen
Nancy Drew
lately?

Nancy Drew has become a girl of the 80s! There is hardly a girl from seven to seventeen who doesn't know her name. Now you can continue to enjoy Nancy Drew in a new series, written for older readers – THE NANCY DREW FILES. Each book has more romance, fashion, mystery and adventure.

Join Nancy in all these fabulous adventures, available only in Armada.

ARMADA

All these books are available at your local bookshop or newsagent, or can be ordered from the publisher. To order direct from the publishers just tick the title you want and fill in the form below:

Name _____

Address _____

_____

Send to: Collins Childrens Cash Sales
          PO Box 11
          Falmouth
          Cornwall
          TR10 9EN

Please enclose a cheque or postal order or debit my Visa/ Access –

   Credit card no:

   Expiry date:

   Signature:

– to the value of the cover price plus:

UK: 60p for the first book, 25p for the second book, plus 15p per copy for each additional book ordered to a maximum charge of £1.90.

BFPO: 60p for the first book, 25p for the second book plus 15p per copy for the next 7 books, thereafter 9p per book.

Overseas and Eire: £1.25 for the first book, 75p for the second book. Thereafter 28p per book.

Armada reserve the right to show new retail prices on covers which may differ from those previously advertised in the text or elswhere.

ARMADA